Masquerade

A Fetish & Fantasy Novella

Lori King

Edited by: Ekatarina Sayanova
Red Quill Editing, LLC
Artwork by: Jess Buffett
Jess Buffett Graphic Designs
Photography by: Royal Touch Photography
Model: Sidda Lee Rain

Published by: Lori King Books

Blurb

One night.

Two people.

One risky move.

Can a submissive find happiness being auctioned off to a Dom she only knows as a business associate

Can a Dominant chance creating a bond with a brand new submissive when he's determined to stay a bachelor?

When the mask is lifted away, and both of them are exposed, can they seek comfort from each other and experience their secret fantasies? Or will they back away for fear of "what if"?

Fetish & Fantasy Series
Watching Sin
Submission Dance
Mistress Hedonism
Masquerade

Dedication

This book is specifically for my author friends. We live behind the computer screen in our pajama pants and bathrobes. Our hair isn't styled, our makeup isn't neatly applied, and we survive on caffeine and positive reviews, but we keep marching forward against the current. We keep striving for deeper, more emotional stories that tear our readers down and build them back up, because our soul has come to crave the creation. In a sometimes lonely career, it's wonderful to have friends I can lean on. So for my regular cohorts in crime: Bryce Evans, Elle Boon, Caitlyn O'Leary, and KD Jones, this book is for you guys and the many others. Because you guys keep me from ripping out my hair, bashing in the computer screen, or just running away to Tibet to climb a mountain and hide from technology. I love you guys more than words can say. Keep writing.

Lori

Chapter One

The fragrance of leather and sandalwood filled Julia's nose, and she drew it deep into her lungs, letting it soothe her. There was something comforting about the space that had brought her so much pleasure and pain. She knew it would seem odd to some people that she needed pain to feel free of herself, but after years of avoiding her demons, she found it particularly cathartic to face them head-on while strapped to a spanking bench.

Although her nerves were rattling around in her belly, she marched into the massive house as though she knew what she was doing. She'd learned years ago that confidence was the best bluff there was, and most people would ignore someone who looked as if they belonged. No one seeing her would ever guess how out of her element she felt tonight. It wasn't the house or even the crowd that filled it. It was the anticipation and apprehension of what the night could bring that put her on edge. Music reached her ears as she entered the main foyer, and she was greeted by a friendly smile.

"Julia! You look smoking hot tonight!" Natasha's braided pigtails bounced on her shoulders as she rushed over for a hug. Julia accepted the embrace even though she wasn't a particularly touchy-feely person. After six months of taking classes with the other woman, she felt as close to her as anyone.

"Thanks, Natasha. You do, too. Love the mask."

The monthly Lusty Fantasies fetish party was generally a less dressy affair, but it was Halloween, and Killian Whitfield had gone all out to ensure his guests would have a magical time. The theme was a masquerade, so each guest was encouraged to wear a mask. Julia had selected a lacy black piece with just the smallest bit of sparkly embellishment, because it set off her green eyes and pale skin. Meanwhile, Natasha had picked a pink mask with feathers curling around her left cheek; it paired perfectly with her baby doll nightie and pigtails.

"It took me forever to pick out my outfit for tonight, and my tummy is in a knot. I'm so nervous about the auction." Natasha and Julia were two of the six submissives who were being graduated out of a submissives training course. Normally, this would just mean they now had full rights as submissives within the party boundaries, but tonight they were celebrating in a spectacularly public fashion. They were being auctioned off for charity.

"Master Killian wouldn't let anything bad happen to us. I know he vetted all of the people that will be bidding tonight, and eliminated ones who wouldn't suit," Julia responded, waving off her friend's fears in spite of her own anxiety. The idea of being free from the restrictions her status as a submissive virgin put on her was great, but knowing that she now had no one making decisions for her while she was at these parties was intimidating.

In real life, Julia Sweet was the CEO of her own company. She had employees, clients, business meetings, and extensive responsibilities, but when she was at a Lusty Fantasies event, she could let all of that go. For the last six months, it had been wonderful to not worry about anything except following instructions when she entered this house. She'd really enjoyed all of the various demonstrations and scenes she'd been allowed to experience, but she hadn't really considered what would happen when the classes were over. She didn't have a regular Top lined up to take care of her needs, and if she didn't find one she could trust, she'd find herself right back where she was six months ago. Wound up tighter than a bow string, and unsatisfied.

In her mind's eye, she saw a flash of golden blonde hair, and piercing blue eyes, but she forced the image away just as quickly. Ashton Reid wasn't an option. Not only was he a well-trained, extremely experienced Master to her novice status, but she also had business dealings with him, and she sat on the boards of several charitable organizations alongside him.

A glorious piece of man flesh, Ashton stood at nearly six foot four, but it was the aura of power and control he carried, paired with his playful charm that stole the hearts of every woman he met. He'd certainly stolen hers long before she'd done a scene with him, yet she continued to keep him at arm's length, because he was a notorious playboy. That was most certainly not what she needed in her life. No matter how desirable he was, she needed to stop thinking about him.

"I'm more worried about what happens if no one bids on me!" Natasha said, giggling like a young girl. Natasha's quest to find the perfect Daddy Dom was well known around their group, and she was likely to find several suitors looking to win her tonight. Although Julia knew it was her friend's preference to maintain a childlike appearance and demeanor when she was in her submissive role, it got annoying after a while.

"You have no need to worry. I plan on winning you for myself tonight."

Turning to face the deep voice, Julia was surprised to see one of the long-time members addressing Natasha. Edwin North was nearly twenty years older than Julia, making him another decade older than Natasha, but he looked at the younger woman like she was an angel from heaven.

Natasha giggled, and dipped her head as she cheeks flushed, "Thank you, Sir. I would like that very much."

"You would, would you? Tell me girl, how shall you reward me when I win your collar tonight?" Edwin asked. He still stood a few feet away, maintaining a comfortable distance while he directed his question to Natasha, but the strength of his dominance could be felt in the air around them.

"Oh, Sir, I'd be so relieved to have been purchased by someone I respected, I'd do anything you asked of me," Natasha said with another annoying giggle.

How many times could one woman giggle before someone slapped her? It was a question Julia had considered more than once since meeting the girl.

"If you'll both excuse me." Julia glanced back at Edwin only to realize neither of the two had any idea she was still standing there in the first place. She hadn't even realized the couple had formed a bond, but it was certainly understandable. Edwin had played a large part in their submissive training classes; he was one of the few experienced Dominants in their circle who had trained extensively in multiple kinks. He'd taught them about furries and pony play, and, of course, Daddy/baby play. Come to think of it, Natasha had been his volunteer for that particular demonstration. That was likely when the two had hit it off.

Edwin had also been the one to explore impact play with each submissive during their first month of training, and later, he'd been the one to test their interest in anal play as well. Natasha was the only submissive that had shown interest in all of the kinks he offered up, but per Killian's rules, they were all expected to attend and participate in scenes that included each brand of play. The idea was to immerse them in the various forms kinks, and let them find what truly appealed to their inner submissive. Some things came naturally, while others weren't even tolerable. There were a few things off limits within the Lusty Fantasies club parties: any kind of waste play, blood play, fire play, and after a recent scare, breath play had also been added to the banned activities list.

None of those forbidden items appealed to her, thankfully. Julia was content to experience a little of every taboo pleasure they'd shown her, and in doing so, she'd found a few that surprised her. Most important was the one wax play scene she'd experienced. It had been more thrilling than she could have ever imagined, yet she still wasn't sure if that was due to the actual play, or the Master involved.

Her mind circled back to the night she'd been under Master Ashton's hand as he expertly painted her body with dripping wax. It was a Friday evening so the only people around were the submissive trainees and Tops giving demonstrations. Julia and the other submissives had all been assigned to view specific scenes. Usually, one sub was chosen to participate while the rest watched, and if there was time, the Top would offer up his or her services to others later.

That night, Julia had felt a sense of euphoria when she walked into the bedroom her group was assigned to and found Master Ashton preparing his tools. The queen size bed was draped in a heavy white cloth to protect it, and the lights were off. The entire room was lit with blazing taper candles, and the ambiance instantly brought a feeling of peace to her soul. His eyes met hers even before the other subs had taken their seats on the opposite side of the bed, and she knew he'd ask her to be his bottom for the evening.

She never once second-guessed her agreement to participate in the scene, and she realized then there was something about the playful man that appealed to her deeply. She attributed her reactions to submissive's euphoria—an attraction and subtle bond of trust between any bottom and their Top. In order to bottom for someone, trust was imperative, and that meant forming a connection. She'd felt an unusual connection with Ashton Reid from the first time she laid eyes on him almost three years ago at a board meeting in Houston. They hadn't been introduced at the time, and she hadn't understood her own needs back then.

Not that it mattered. As a neophyte submissive, the likelihood of Ashton Reid wanting her was slim to none, and she needed to be open to other options. At tonight's auction she would be paired up with a Top who truly wanted her enough to commit to donating a small fortune to charity in order to have her. That had to mean something.

Forcing her spine a bit straighter, she moved forward through the party, determined to enjoy the freedom her new status gave her. Here and there were people she'd met who greeted her pleasantly. She liked the fact that, even though she was a submissive, she wasn't expected to submit to everyone. Submission was earned, which meant she only knelt or dropped her eyes for certain people. One of whom was walking her way.

"Hello Julia, you look lovely this evening." Killian Whitfield was a powerful man in business and in life. He commanded the very air around him, but he did so with such a laid back, easy manner people rarely knew he was orchestrating their behavior.

"Thank you Master Killian, as do you." Julia noticed Killian's partner's walking just behind him. "Hello Doug, Alana. I love your dress."

Alana's face lit up, and Julia returned the grin. "Thanks! The guys weren't sure about my plan for our costumes, but I think they turned out great."

Killian wore a black silk shirt over his black slacks, and instead of a mask, his face was elaborately painted with a filigreed design in black red and white. Doug was his opposite, in all white but with the exact same design on his face, while Alana wore an opaque, strapless red sheath that looked more like a thin towel around her than a dress. When she moved, the garment shimmered in the light, and gave just a hint of the dangerous curves underneath. Her face was also painted black, red, and white, but the design was just a bit different—more feminine. Together they were a beautiful sight.

Smiling at his girlfriend, Killian reached out and wrapped his hand around the base of Alana's neck. "You did wonderfully, love. I'm sure we're the envy of all."

Julia had always liked Alana, but their first meeting had been tense. A few years ago, when Killian was still single, he and Julia had enjoyed each other more than once. In fact, it was Killian who had opened her eyes to BDSM in the first place, but it had taken her a long time before she became brave enough to reach out and ask for more information. By that time, Killian was happily ensconced in his current polyamorous relationship with Alana and her husband Doug, but Killian had still welcomed her into the fold. To her surprise, he invited her out to dinner with the three of them and very bluntly laid out the facts of their past relationship to his partners.

Initially, Alana had seemed stunned and angry, but Julia corroborated his story, explaining that there was nothing between the two of them any longer outside of friendship. As they'd delved into discussions that involved BDSM and the D/s lifestyle, Julia had clicked with Alana, and they'd been friends since.

"Are you prepared for the evenings activities?" Killian asked, changing the subject. Julia turned to meet his gaze only to lower her eyes almost instantly. In business she held her own, but here, on his turf, he was king.

"I believe so, yes. I'm a bit nervous, but that's to be expected I'm sure," she answered honestly, giving a sharp nod.

"Of course, but you've nothing to worry about. I've verified all of the bidders myself, and I believe you'll be quite pleased no matter who wins your collar for the evening." He sounded so self-assured that anyone who didn't know him might think him smug, but Julia knew that he was justifiably confident in himself.

"Will you be participating tonight Master Killian?"

Behind him Doug snorted out a laugh, and muttered under his breath, "Not if he's smart."

His sarcasm was cut short by a sharp look from his Master who addressed her, even while clearly scolding his sub with his silence. "Until just this moment, I hadn't planned on it. In fact, I'd planned on being the auctioneer." He paused, and Julia saw Doug swallow hard. "I believe I might reconsider though. In fact, I am going to go check with a few people and see how many bidders we have. Alana, love, would you please take Doug downstairs and set him up on the cross? I believe he needs a few moments of quiet time before he apologizes to me for his assumption."

"Yes, Sir," Alana said, with just a bit too much glee in her tone. Julia nearly laughed at the matching spark of anticipation in Doug's eyes, but she held it in.

"If you'll excuse me, Julia, I have some things to do. Good luck tonight, and don't forget to enjoy yourself." He left her standing in the massive hallway watching his tall form walk away. Killian really was quite a specimen with long muscular limbs, and a golden surfer boy look. If it wasn't for the edge of danger he gave off, one might assume he was less than intelligent, but she knew that he had an IQ that was off the charts, and charisma that served him supremely well in business. It was why she'd chosen him and his company when she was seeking investors for her business, and why she'd ultimately brought him on as a full partner. It was also why she trusted him with her secret desires and signed on for his training classes.

Chapter Two

"Did you plan it like that, or did it just happen organically?"

Ashton pretended not to hear the question as he continued prepping the makeshift stage in the middle of the living room. He wasn't interested in hearing how Madame Belle managed to shave the hair on her pet, Xander so that it looked like he had a tree of hair growing out of his groin and up over his pecs. In his opinion, it looked grotesque, but his opinion didn't matter. In this environment everyone was encouraged to explore their kinks, even if it was something wild like artistic shaving. Hell, more than once people had looked at him askance when they found out he liked to paint his submissives with hot wax, so he wasn't one to judge.

"I didn't start out with a plan, it just sort of grew." Madame Belle was a woman in her sixties, and her playmate was just barely legal. It had initially been a point of contention when she'd asked for a key from Killian to bring Xander along, but per the rules, as long as he signed the correct documents and waivers he was allowed in under her invitation. "Pun intended."

Cackling with her friend, Madame Belle waved her pet to kneel in front of her, and promptly lifted her feet into his lap. Xander looked far from embarrassed or indignant at the move, as he quickly cupped her small feet in his hands and began gently massaging them. The two were polar opposites, and yet they somehow suited each other perfectly.

A tiny twinge of jealousy burned inside Ashton's gut. He craved a partner that fit him like that. It wasn't like he hadn't had a sub, but he'd never quite found that right woman. Someone who needed him just as much as he needed her.

As the thought cleared his brain, his eyes landed on the lush figure of Julia Sweet, and his cock thickened in his leathers. She was exquisite and as feisty in the daylight as she was submissive after dark. He expected she'd make a wonderfully unpredictable sub, and to top it off, she'd look sexy as hell wearing a collar. Something in white gold with an emerald would set off her eyes.

Damn it all, the last thing he needed was a virgin sub in his bed. Even if that full bodied woman turned him on like no one had in years. She had the most beautiful tits he'd ever seen, with mouthwatering pink nipples that hardened up whenever he drew close. He'd only had her naked once, but he'd never forget the sight.

He had always done the wax play demonstrations for the subs in training, but he'd never experienced anything so emotionally unsettling as that one night when Julia had been his guinea pig. She'd seemed skittish at first, but she'd nodded her agreement when he'd asked her to be his volunteer. Once stripped of her clothing, she'd stood proudly before him and the other submissives without flinching. In the general population, she would be considered plus sized, but in his mind, she was perfect. He loved the way her waist dipped in, and then rounded out into wide hips and a plump ass, and her thick thighs hid a lush pussy. Granted, he hadn't had a chance to touch her there, because the scene they'd been doing was all about the sensation of wax, but he remembered the scent of her desire that night. It had been all he could do not to rip his leathers open and slam his cock into her sweetness in front of everyone.

A loud laugh near him drew him out of his dirty thoughts, and he clenched his teeth in frustration. His cock pressed tightly against the metal zipper in his pants, and he had to shift his stance before he turned back to what he was doing.

Julia was beautiful, and intelligent, and absolutely not for him. She needed a sweeter Top. One who was willing to move slowly, and ease her into his demands. That wasn't Ashton's style. He wanted what he wanted, and while he was willing to seduce, once the woman agreed, he expected her submission. He liked to push subs' boundaries and make them squirm. It was pretty black and white in his book, and it didn't leave room for teaching virgins.

"This is perfect, Ashton." Killian's voice drew him out of his wild thoughts, and he looked up at his friend and boss. They'd met in college as frat brothers, and unlike most people, they'd stayed close. When Killian hit it big in business, he extended a job offer to Ashton, and together they'd built Whitfield Industries into a billion dollar company. He could never repay the man for that one defining moment in life, but he'd done his best to be his right hand whenever possible.

Surveying his work, Ashton smiled back at Killian. "Thanks. I figured you'd want to put them on display as if they were actual merchandise, and this seemed like the best way to do it. If they're right here in the center of the room everyone can see every inch of them. Do you plan on displaying them naked?"

"No I don't think so. I've no doubt the sight of these subs will cause a bidding frenzy even in their clothes," Killian said with a chuckle. "Actually, that's something I wanted to talk to you about. Do you have a minute?"

Lifting his tool bag, Ashton brushed his wrist over his forehead to clear away the sweat and followed Killian away from the crowded living room. He stopped long enough to stow the bag in a hall closet where it could be found when needed before they continued on to Killian's office. With a heavy sigh, he flopped down in a leather armchair.

"What's up boss?"

Killian, propped himself on the edge of the desk and folded his arms. "I assume you're familiar with the list of virgins in the auction tonight?"

Ashton shook his head. "Nah, I wasn't planning on bidding, so I didn't bother. Why?"

"Why aren't you bidding?"

"The last thing I need is a scared bunny in my bed," Ashton said with a laugh. "When I want to play, I much prefer experience and confidence over traumatizing a neophyte."

"I see; well, then, you won't mind helping me out."

Quirking one eyebrow in question, Ashton felt his breath catch. Killian always got that look on his face when he had a plan for something, and his plans always seemed to work in his favor.

"Doug and Alana need my attention this evening. We've had a trying couple of weeks with the Gaff's Venture buyout, and Doug's been acting out more than I like. If I don't rein him in now I won't be able to proceed with my plans over Christmas for the three of us. I'd planned on acting as the auctioneer for tonight's festivities, but I believe they need me more. I'd like for you to take over."

"You want me to be the auctioneer?" Ashton asked skeptically. "What would I have to do exactly?"

"I have diagrammed out the list of potential bidders for each virgin so that we can be sure that they're purchased by individuals with their best interests at heart. The bidding part will be silent, so no one will know who is bidding on whom. That way none of our merchandise gets their feelings hurt if the Dominant of their choice bids for someone else."

"Okay...and?"

"I need you to review the bids and select the correct bidder to win each virgin."

Ashton stared at Killian in surprise, "Wait, so they're not going to the highest bidder?"

"Not necessarily. As much as I want to help our charity, I also want to take care of our subs. That means making a choice that's best for each of them, even if that choice was outbid. No one but you and I will know the truth of the bids." Killian reached across the desk and took a folder out of the drawer, handing it to Ashton.

"You sketchy bastard. Why am I not surprised?"

Killian gave him a smug shrug, and waited silently.

Flipping the folder open, he stared down at the cocky grin of the woman he'd spent nights dreaming about. Her pink lips curved up, and one eyebrow was cocked in a sassy come-and-get-me look that made his balls ache. Julia was one of the subs being auctioned off. Tonight, she would submit to a man in every way, and it wouldn't be him.

With Killian still watching him closely, he reviewed his options. He knew there was no getting out of this task, but could he really auction Julia off to another Dom?

"I'll do it, but only because I've been on the butt end of Doug's pissy mood before. You go handle your business. I've got this." He attempted to throw his swagger into his voice. He'd covered many weaknesses with confidence before, and he'd be damned if a virgin sub was going to distract him from this. At least as the auctioneer, he'd have a choice on who she ended up with.

Killian gave him an odd look and then said, "Good, that's settled. I'll be in the dungeon if you need me." He stood and pinched the bridge of his nose for a moment before rolling his eyes. "Damn makeup. I'm going to stripe Alana's ass for making me wear it."

"Wasn't the masquerade theme your idea?" Ashton teased.

"Shut up." Grumbling under his breath Killian disappeared into the connected bathroom leaving Ashton alone with the folder that held his heart. How was he going to get through this without scooping Julia up like a caveman and carting her away to a locked bedroom?

Chapter Three

Staring at the list of six virgins to be auctioned off, it took all of fifteen minutes for Ashton to realize he was in serious trouble. The men vying for Julia's collar were not suitable at all, in his opinion.

Looking at her list of limits and interests, he noted that she'd marked only four items with a ten out of ten on her desires list. That wasn't unusual for a new sub. She was most likely still nervous about experiencing new things. Watching demonstrations was different than actual submission. Her top three were fairly mundane: open-handed spanking, bondage, and hair pulling. The one that intrigued him was her interest in wax play. He wanted to believe it was thanks to his fabulous skill in demonstrating it, but more than likely, she'd just found a kink she enjoyed. It wouldn't be fair for him to assume she wanted him to go along with it.

And he was lying to himself if he thought he could stomach handing her over to another man. Especially for a price. That would feel completely wrong.

Seriously, Reid. Get over yourself. She signed up for this because she wanted it. Cursing his own inner turmoil, he flipped through the other lists and quickly realized that there was one stand-out Dominant for each submissive. In each instance, one person who suited the sub's needs more than anyone else—except for Julia.

Not one of her suitors matched her initial desires, and in some cases, they preferred play that included some of her hard limits. The most obvious choice was Timar Said, a visiting Master from another state who had been coming to their events for several months. Ashton didn't know much about the man outside of his business dealings with Killian, but he did know that Timar was a generous Dominant with a significant amount of experience in training virgins. He also knew that the man had a preference for male submissives, and it piqued his curiosity to see him suddenly seeking out a female.

Full of questions, Ashton took the file Killian had given him, and left the office feeling unsettled. He had some serious thinking to do before he settled on a solution to his dilemma. After all, Julia's entire night was balanced on him making the right decision.

~ ~ ~

Julia's nerves grew more taut with every minute that passed. The auction was due to begin in the next thirty minutes, and she'd had second, third, and fourth thoughts about doing it. She could always back out. Killian wouldn't think badly of her, but she wouldn't feel good about it herself. She needed to find a Top who could help her, and in this case, she would at least know that the person winning her was safe, sane, and wanted her. That was more than she'd get finding someone at a bar to take home for the night.

She spent up to twelve hours a day making decisions that effected people's livelihoods. The weight of the world seemed to be sitting on her shoulders every evening as she made her way home. The need for release was a constant barrier to finding a meaningful relationship. It wasn't that she wanted someone to step in and take over her life for her, but she desperately wanted someone in her life she could lean on, a soft place to fall. In her submission, she felt free, like she could float away on a breeze, and she craved that weightless feeling like a drug. The more she experienced it, the harder it got to go home after a training session or a party alone.

"Hey Julia, can I borrow you for a moment?" Master Daniel found her hiding out in the partially concealed alcove. Daniel and his submissive, Kitty, were party regulars, and he was proficient in Shibari. He'd done several demonstrations involving various forms of bondage, and Julia had a weak spot for him. Not that it would have mattered who was asking. She also had a soft heart and rarely said no when asked for help.

"Of course, Master Daniel." Forcing her feet to move, she stepped further into the light where he held out his hand for her to take.

"Thank you, precious. I promise I won't take up much of your time. I just need an extra pair of hands for a moment."

Her expression concerned, she hurried after him as he led her into one of the bedrooms where Kitty lay on a massive bed, tied in a beautiful pattern of colorful ropes. A roll of heavy-duty plastic wrap sat on the floor, and strips of it were scattered on the bed. The woman was clearly deep in subspace, and Julia looked at Daniel in question.

"I need to get her into the tub and try to wake her up a bit, but I'm concerned she'll come out of it while I'm trying to cut the ropes. If you'll hold her still, I'll have her out quickly."

Julia could hear the worry in Daniel's tone, and she felt her respect for the man grow. He clearly cared deeply for Kitty, and if he was worried, she was, too.

"Is this normal for her?"

Daniel shook his head, "Not really. She goes deep, but not usually that fast, and I can always get a response from her even when she's in subspace." He quickly slit the ropes as Julia braced the woman with her weight to ensure her safety. Once Kitty was free of the restraint, Daniel scooped her up in his arms and hurried toward the attached bathroom.

Each of the bedrooms in Killian's house had massive bathrooms attached with specific features that only someone in the BDSM community would notice. In this one the tub was sunk into the floor, and there were several mounts where someone could be restrained for play. Tonight Daniel wasn't wasting any time with his aftercare, and while Julia watched from the doorway, he stepped into the empty tub still dressed in dark slacks and carrying his submissive, and took a seat on the bench.

"Do you need anything else, Master Daniel? Should I call for help?" Julia asked as he turned on the tap, and the water began filling the basin, soaking his clothes, and submerging the couple.

"No, thank you, Julia. I'm sure she'll be fine shortly. The water should help bring her around faster." He nuzzled the hair on top of Kitty's head, and Julia felt a pang of jealousy at the affectionate gesture. She turned to leave them alone, when he called out again. "Julia, on second thought, would you send one of the other Masters in? I'm supposed to take a DM shift later tonight, and I'm going to need them to cover me."

"Of course." She nodded and hurried out of the bedroom and ran smack dab into the broad chest of the man she'd most wanted to see tonight.

"Whoa! Where's the fire?" Ashton asked, bracing her to keep her upright. He held a file of papers in one hand, and somehow managed to hold her with the other. "Julia? Is everything okay?"

~ ~ ~

Ashton tried not to wrap the lush woman in his arms when she plowed into him. He knew instantly whom he held, and it took everything he had not to drop the paperwork in his hand and hold her tight.

"I need you," Julia said shortly, spinning and grabbing his hand to pull him along behind her into the bedroom.

His heart lurched at her words, and he silently wondered if it was possible to stroke out because of intense desire. He wanted to question her, but within a moment, they were stepping into the bathroom. His protective instinct kicked in when he saw Daniel cradling a pale Kitty in his arms.

"What happened?" he asked sharply, hurrying to the edge of the tub. He reached out instinctively to feel for her pulse. Daniel gave him a death glare and clenched his jaw at the move. A collared submissive was generally off limits to everyone without their Dominant's permission, but this was a special circumstance.

"She went too deep, but Julia helped me get her loose and in the tub. I think she's coming around now, but I'll need someone to cover my DM shift at one," Daniel explained.

Ashton nodded. "Of course, consider it done. I'll have Tex take your shift, and if she's doing okay, you can have his five a.m. shift. If not, I'll cover it. What sent her so deep?"

"I'm not sure." Daniel said shaking his head. "We were trying something new, and we'd barely gotten started."

"Something new?" Ashton asked with a frown.

"Mummification and I barely got the first layer of wraps on her legs before she slipped into subspace. I switched gears and worked the ropes to lighten the sensation, but she just kept getting deeper."

"Did she pass out or just get spacey?"

"She was spacey, and then she stopped responding, and I went for help. Julia just happened to be at the right place at the right time." Daniel gave Julia a smile that set Ashton's teeth on edge. "Thank you again, precious."

"Of course. Anytime." She returned the bright smile with one of her own. Ashton's cock twitched to life, and he gave a mental curse. That was not what he needed right now. He was still working on a solution to the auction problem, and he'd literally just come up with a plan when he ran into Julia. The auction was supposed to start soon, and he needed to talk to someone beforehand. "I hope Kitty is okay, Master Daniel."

"S'good." Kitty mumbled, turning her face into the crook of Daniel's neck. Relieved sighs echoed through the room, and Ashton rose to his feet with a nod.

"It looks like she'll be fine. Let me know if you need anything else," he told Daniel, whose sole focus was now on his submissive. Turning away from the tableau in front of him, Ashton went to Julia and nudged her out of the bathroom.

"They need some privacy for a bit," he told her, letting his hand run up her spine to the back of her neck as he walked her back out of the room. He turned and pulled the door shut, double-checking that a pair of bracelets hung on the knob. It was a universal party signal that the people inside weren't to be disturbed.

"Are you sure one of us shouldn't stay just in case they need something else?" Julia asked, concern making her forehead wrinkle. She looked so cute that Ashton couldn't resist running his fingertip over the tiny line between her eyebrows.

"They're just fine, little one. Daniel knows what Kitty needs. If she doesn't perk up pretty quickly he'll stop at nothing to get her to a doctor."

After another moment of hesitation she finally nodded her agreement and turned away from the closed door. It was in that moment that she seemed to realize they were standing so close to one another, and she took a wobbly step backward.

"The auction should be starting soon. I'd better get in there." She turned away so that her beautiful breasts were out of view, but her perfect heart shaped ass now held his attention.

"No rush. They can't start without me. I'm the auctioneer."

Her face paled and she froze in motion. "What do you mean? I thought Killian was handling the auction."

He frowned at the lack of respect in her tone, but let it slide. She obviously had strong feelings about the auction. He was hoping for her sake it was just nerves.

"Killian needed to step away, and he asked me to take over. Don't worry, little one, I won't let any big bad wolves eat you for a midnight snack." She flushed at his teasing, and her eyes dropped submissively.

"I'm sorry, Master Ashton. I shouldn't have questioned Master Killian's decision. I'm just a bit on edge. Forgive me."

He let himself run his hand over her hair, and smiled as she fought to hold still under his touch. "Forgiven, this time. Next time I'll be sure to turn that pretty ass bright red. Tell me, are you on edge because you want someone specific to win you tonight?"

"No, Sir. I'm just not a fan of the unknown. I prefer to have a plan and execute it with logic and organization. Auctions aren't logical. Sure, the winner is the highest bidder, but that might not be the person with the most money to spend. Sometimes it's just the person with the most to lose."

Surprised at the insightful answer, Ashton could only watch as Julia scurried off down the hall and disappeared into the living room. She was right. Tonight, one person had more to lose than anyone else, and he was damn sure going to see that she came out the winner.

Chapter Four

The wooden platform under her bare knees was cold. Goose-bumps rose on her arms and legs, but Julia wasn't sure if it was from the temperature, or all of the eyes on her. The party guests milled around chatting as if nothing unusual was happening, even with six submissives kneeling in the middle of the room.

When she reached the living room, she was embarrassed to realize she was the last one to arrive, and she'd hurried to take the last open space on the small stage. It lifted them about eighteen inches off the ground, so that they were fairly visible to everyone in the room. Kneeling on the very end of the line of six, Julia was especially vulnerable to view. It wasn't that she minded people looking her way—she was used to having people stare at her because of her fuller figure—

but knowing they were each thinking about her sexually made her entire body tingle with desire.

There was a sense of anticipation in the air, and when Ashton finally appeared to commence taking bids, the crowd cheered.

"Simmer down people. I had to handle some business, but I know you're all anxious to get started." He made his way through the packed room and took a position just to Julia's left. If she reached out, she'd be able to touch him, to ground herself in reality for a just a moment before fantasy took over again, but that wasn't appropriate. Committing herself more fully, she stared down at her knees, and drew invisible lines between the small, dark freckles on her thighs to stay focused.

"I know you've all read the rules or you wouldn't be here tonight, but I'm going to cover them again just in case. We have six submissives, and over forty bidders. Some of you are going home empty handed." The crowd rumbled with anxious laughter and disappointed sighs, before quieting again. "The minimum bid is ten thousand, and there will only be ten minutes allotted for each item up for bid. If you don't get your bid in to me in time, you're out of luck. Bids are confidential, so only the bidder and I will know how much they purchased their prize for. Once a winner is announced, he or she can take possession of their sub for the next twelve hours. At approximately noon everyone parts ways as friends. If things go well, we'll have the new subs collared by dawn. If things don't go well, I guess we'll serve extra tequila with the mimosas at brunch." His joke lightened the tension just a bit, and Julia admired his charisma in front of the crowd. Ashton was showing his skills at crowd management perfectly. "I'll review the bids and announce the winner as quickly as possible before moving on to the next sub. At the end, I'll tally the total and announce how much we're giving to the local Boys and Girls Club. Sound good?"

Murmurs of agreement and approval filled Julia's ears, but she silently repeated nursery rhymes in her head to avoid slipping from her submissive pose. That infraction would be terrible in this particular situation.

"We'll start on the far end with Derrick. Stand up Derrick, and do a turn for the crowd so that they can see you." Once his request had been complied with, Ashton addressed the crowd again. "You have ten minutes to submit your bids people; don't be late."

Kneeling in this position for any length of time was fairly uncomfortable for anyone, but for Julia in particular it was tough on her knees. As a result of a dislocated knee while playing softball back in high-school, she sometimes found kneeling impossible, so she sent a prayer of thanks up when Ashton leaned over and said softly to the six submissives, "You may all take a seat on your rear until it's your turn."

With a sigh of relief, she stretched her cramping knees out, and let her legs hang over the edge of the platform. Lifting her head instinctively, her eyes clashed with Ashton's before she remembered she wasn't supposed to be making eye contact with anyone and dropped her gaze.

The brief eye contact was enough to make her heart thump harder. He looked at her like he wanted to make a meal of her. A predator with prey in his sights. If only he could place a bid of his own, perhaps... Shaking her head at her own silly thoughts, she went back to silently reciting nursery rhymes and meditating while she awaited her fate.

Hickory dickory dock... The mouse ran up the clock...

~ ~ ~

Ashton could see that Julia was relieved to change positions when she shifted, and he silently congratulated himself for noting her discomfort in the kneeling position. He'd have to remember to check her file for injuries that might inhibit play.

While he waited for bidders to inspect Derrick and finalize their bids, he pulled out her fact sheet and reviewed it. Hayfever, a latex allergy, migraine headaches, and stiff joints were all listed as possible health concerns. The detail he was looking for jumped out at him. She'd been injured as a teenager, and her knee gave her troubles when it was bent for too long.

Under normal circumstances a woman might not reveal such unusual medical issues to her sex partners, but in BDSM every possible outcome was planned for. A latex allergy meant certain types of toys and condoms had to be used to protect her from a terribly uncomfortable reaction. Migraines could indicate a blood pressure problem, and it would be important for her Top to ensure she was feeling okay after sustained play. And the stiff joints and knee injury explained why she disliked the standard submissive pose. It could also inhibit certain activities like a kneeling bench, crawling, and being tied up for too long.

Before he could read further into her file, bidders began approaching him with their sealed envelopes, and he had to focus on his job. It didn't take long for him to realize the benefit to silent bids. Some of the bidders were grossly undervaluing their potential subs, while others were just throwing money at the auction. Not surprisingly, each person that Killian had pre-selected for the submissive was well within a generous, but not ridiculous amount. Selecting winners was going to be simple.

Lifting his head as the timer went off signaling the end of the first bidding round, he noticed a young guy named Brandon Grant stroking Julia's hair and whispering to her.

Rage and indignation filled his chest and he snapped. "No touching the merchandise unless you own it, Grant."

Brandon lifted his arrogant gaze to Ashton's and said, "I'm sure I'll own it soon enough."

Ashton had to bite back a snappy retort. It wouldn't do for the true manner of this auction to be revealed, even if it would shove Brandon's cocky attitude up his ass. No, he had to let the man go, and just ignore him.

Brandon had been on probation for almost three full months after sending his bottom, Lilyann to the hospital with a mild concussion. That put him at the top of Ashton's shit list. He would gladly throw himself into the ring to protect any sub from Brandon's harsh touch, but he knew many of the party goers were actually pain sluts who preferred the other man's ways. That was the only reason Killian allowed him to keep his Dominant status. He'd been forced to retake a few classes on how to handle impact play and submissive aftercare, but once he'd passed those requirements, he was allowed back at the parties. Now he'd set his sights on Ashton's woman.

Heart tripping, Ashton's eyes shot to Julia. What was he thinking? She wasn't his woman. Hell, he wasn't even sure if his plan would work. And if it did, how would she feel about him twelve hours from now? Most likely she'd be furious because he'd duped her.

"Who's the winner, Ash?" Mason Allen called out from the back of the room, startling Ashton from his musings.

Smiling at the crowd apologetically, he shook his head, "Sorry everyone, I got caught daydreaming. Looks like the winner is…" pausing for dramatic affect as he pretended to review the cards again, he took a deep breath and announced, "Mason Allen!"

A whoop went up from the black man, and he shot forward toward the stage. "Damn right I'm the winner. I knew this sub was mine six months ago. We just had to get all the details out of the way."

Mason was a friend of Ashton's, so he knew the man's kinks pretty well, and he was one hundred percent sure that Killian had made the right call on this pairing. The way Derrick smiled back at Mason as he stepped off the stage, and accepted the other man's bracelet on his wrist just cemented the feeling. The bracelets signified an attachment or claim of sorts at a Lusty Fantasies party. Only individuals who had completed the Masters training course were allowed to have a set. The black band was worn by the Top, while the white was given to his bottom. In some cases it was just for the night, and in other cases it was exchanged for a permanent collar or some other jewelry or mark denoting their commitment.

"Well done, Mason. Killian will be collecting a check from you. Enjoy your prize." Ashton said, gesturing the pair away. Catcalls followed them as Mason led Derrick out of the crowded room and disappeared into the hallway. Each submissive had been assigned a room for the night, and the Tops bidding had to agree to stay in the residence in order to get bidding privileges. This way, there was a Dungeon Monitor within hearing distance. It was just one more layer of protection Killian put in place for the submissives he trained.

"Let's move on, shall we? Next up is Natasha, our very own baby-girl." He arched his brow at the woman in question when he looked over and caught her staring his way. Immediately, her cheeks turned pink and she dropped her head. "Stand up Natasha so that we can see that pretty nightie."

Giggling, the girl rose to her feet and spun in a dainty circle so that she could be admired from all sides. Bidding for her was hot and heavy, but her collar ultimately went to Master Edwin. The older man seemed just as excited—if less vocal—about his win when he collected his prize. When he approached the stage, he presented Natasha with a bracelet as well as a delicate looking hair bow that she squealed over.

Laughing at the antics, the crowd watched the pair leave the room, and then turned back to the stage. Tensions rose as two more subs were auctioned off, leaving only Julia and one other on stage.

"Creighton is next, and he's got a penchant for being bratty, so he'll need a strong hand to keep him in line. Who's up for the task?" Ashton asked the crowd, who loudly responded with jokes and innuendos as bids began stacking up. In the end, Creighton went to a Domme named Leslie Gonzales, who immediately locked his hands and feet in shackles, and latched a leash to the chain before strutting him out of the room. Everything was going as planned, but the biggest hurdle was yet to come.

"Last but definitely not least, is the beautiful Julia."

Without being directed, Julia rose to her feet, and spun for the crowd. He watched her in silence, and wondered at the distant look in her eyes. It was almost as if she'd shut down while she was on stage and blocked everyone out. It wasn't unusual for a sub to distance themselves when they were uncomfortable, but the idea that she'd put herself in a position she was uncomfortable in made him angry.

"Look up at the crowd, Julia, let them see those sexy lips in a smile." He instructed. She jerked in surprise, and then gave a shaky smile to the room before dropping her eyes again. His desire to protect nearly overrode his good sense when she rolled her shoulders forward as if trying to fold in on herself. Why in the world did she put herself in this position if it wasn't what she wanted?

Shaking off the urge to throw her over his shoulder and cart her off for a good spanking, he gestured to the crowd and barked out, "Ten minutes folks."

The bids poured in, but he was only looking for one. When it finally appeared in front of him, he looked up into the eyes of one of his good friends nonchalantly and gave a nod of thanks.

Lex Gregory's lip curled up, but he returned the nod without a word before returning to his seat, and pulling his girlfriend, Marley, into his lap. Ashton wasn't certain how people would react to the monogamous Lex bidding on Julia all of a sudden, but he tried not to let his nerves show on his face as he accepted the rest of the bids. Lex was doing him a solid, and he was grateful.

He tried not to think about the fact that Timar had yet to place a bid, but still he caught himself watching the man out of the corner of his eye. When Brandon Grant marched up to the podium with an envelope, Ashton couldn't stop a threatening snarl from breaking free.

"How did you get a bidders envelope?" He snapped at the cocky younger man.

Brandon shrugged, and gave him a smirk, "Doesn't matter, does it? I've got one, and I know I'm the highest bidder, so take it."

Accepting the envelope without throwing it back at Brandon, was one of the hardest things he'd ever done, but he managed. The minutes flew past and the timer went off signaling the end of the auction. Ashton glanced over at Julia before addressing the crowd, relieved to see her shoulders had lifted and she looked more confident than before.

"That's it. Bidding is over." He paused pretending to review the bids once more before he smiled at the crowd playfully and said, "Wow, you guys either really like our darling Julia, or you're horny as hell tonight."

Laughter rippled through the room, and out of the corner of his eye he noted Julia's tense spine relax slightly. Her anxiety must have been partially fear of being rejected, because now that she knew she was wanted she bore a much stronger stance.

"The winner of the final auction for the night, is…" Lifting the piece of paper that was either his saving grace, or his ticket to hell, he spoke the name written on it. "Master Lex."

There was a moment of surprised silence and then polite applause as everyone really took in the fact that the already claimed Lex had just paid a small fortune for a night with a second sub. Everyone was watching for his girlfriend's reaction, but Marley surprised them all. Looking to Lex for his approval, Marley jumped to her feet and hurried to Julia's side. Her arms wrapped around the other woman, and she whispered something into her ear, before the two, walked to Lex's side.

Lex gave Ashton one more pointed look and then led the two women from sight, leaving a shocked crowd behind for Ashton to handle.

"That's all for tonight. Enjoy the festivities, and be sure to play safe!" he called out to the already dispersing crowd. He had to drop the bid envelopes off in Killian's office before he could put his plan into practice, and now that the ball was rolling so were his doubts.

Brandon stopped him before he could make it out of the room. "That's bullshit. I know I bid higher than Lex."

"Oh? And how do you know that Grant?" He asked, lifting one eyebrow and glaring down his nose at Brandon.

"There's no way he bid more than me. I bid nearly a half a million. Julia should be mine."

"Is there a problem here?" Mistress Ana Gregory, Lex's sister, and another of the longtime group members approached. Ashton had never felt intimidated by a woman before, but Ana looked the part of a badass Domme tonight. He noted Brandon flinching away from her when she stopped by his side.

"I'm just attempting to claim my prize. I know I rightfully won that sub." Brandon grumbled.

"Grant, I've had about enough of you. Killian was nice enough to allow you back to the parties, but that doesn't mean anyone around here has forgotten what happened between you and Lilyann. I would suggest you walk away, and accept that Lex bid higher for Julia than you did." Ana said sharply "Besides, if you choose to pursue calling my brother a liar and a cheat I might have to lose my temper."

Brandon's skin faded to an unusual shade of gray but he acquiesced and stomped away without another word, leaving Ashton to face Ana's questions.

"Do you know why my brother bid on a night with Julia?" Ana asked softly once they were alone.

"I do, but I'd prefer not to discuss it right now. Suffice it to say, Lex is in no way considering being unfaithful to Marley." Ashton responded.

"Good," Ana nodded looking relieved, "I'd have to feed him his balls if he was. Oh, and Ashton, take care of her. I like her."

With that, Ana sauntered back to her submissives, Wyatt and Foster, leaving Ashton to his own devices. He didn't even question how Ana had figured out his game. It didn't matter anymore. He had to get through his DM shift so that he could join his waiting sub in the bedroom Marley was preparing for her.

Chapter Five

Julia's stomach was fluttering, and her knees were shaking hard enough she wasn't sure she would be able to walk, but when the moment finally came, and the winner was announced, she couldn't react. Lex Gregory was the last person she'd ever expected to bid on her, or any other sub for that matter. He was happily ensconced in a relationship with Marley Saltzman, and everyone knew it.

She tried her best not to let her disappointment show when Marley headed her way. She'd hoped for an unattached Top who might be interested in forming a more lasting partnership, but there was no chance of that with Lex. He was likely just looking for a fun night of play. Trying not to think about the fact that she was probably in for her first experience with a woman tonight, she accepted Marley's hug, and barely registered her whispered, "Relax, everything will work out better than you think."

Allowing the other woman to take her hand, she followed the pair out of the crowded living room and up the stairs. When they reached a quiet corner at the top of the massive staircase, Lex turned to face her and her mouth went dry.

Alexander Gregory was the epitome of tall, dark, and handsome. He wore all black to every party, and tonight was no exception. His girlfriend, Marley wore a bright, emerald green corset over a tight, black pair of cheeky shorts that perfectly showed off her curvy figure. They were a beautiful couple, and they had no business bringing her into their bed.

"Why did you buy me?" she snapped, letting her frustration and anxiety get the best of her.

Lex's jaw flexed and his brow furrowed in irritation. "Excuse me? I believe you must have me confused with a less experienced Dom, brat."

Flushing with embarrassment, she dropped her eyes to her feet, and tried not to cry. "I'm sorry, Master Lex. I'm out of sorts. I was so nervous...and I never expected you to...well I mean, you have Marley, and I'm...oh good grief. I'm sorry, Sir."

Tears burned her eyes, but she refused to let them fall. A dark spot on the carpet became her sole focus, and she stared into it as though it were a hole that would grow large enough to swallow her up.

She sensed more than saw, Lex take a deep breath, before his hand came up to cup her jaw, lifting her face. His eyes were a shocking blue color that reminded her of a neon sign from the highway, but they weren't angry. In fact, they looked amused.

"Calm yourself, brat. I didn't purchase you for my own use tonight. I did so for a friend. An anonymous benefactor you might say," Lex explained.

Suddenly her nerves were on high alert and she blurted out, "But Master Killian said only the people he approved were allowed to bid in the auction."

Marley giggled next to her, and Lex shot her a dark look. "I'm going to forgive your manners, brat, because you're clearly having a lapse in training tonight. You're correct that Master Killian vetted all bidders tonight, including the one who now owns your collar for the night. I just happened to be the middleman because the gentleman prefers anonymity. Now, Marley will take you to the room you're assigned to, and prepare you for your Master. Perhaps you'll take the time alone to go through the basics of submission in your head before he has to spank your pretty ass for being such a brat."

Feeling completely thrown off balance, confused, and slightly ashamed at her own behavior, Julia nodded her acceptance and let Marley lead her down the hallway away from Lex. The moment they were out of his sight, Marley wrapped her arm around Julia's shoulder and hugged her close.

"Didn't you hear me tell you it's going to be all right? Sir wouldn't give you to someone he didn't trust completely," Marley assured her.

Julia looked up into the other woman's eyes, and saw the truth there. Feeling a bit more relaxed she asked, "Do you know who it is?"

"Yes, but there's no way I'll risk getting punished by spilling the beans," Marley answered with a grin. "Lex and I are going to play in the dungeon tonight, and I'll be damned if I'm going to have to go without an orgasm to ease your worries."

Julia couldn't blame her, but the refusal didn't help her anxiety. Once inside the bedroom assigned to her, Marley told her to completely strip, and lay down on the bed on a towel.

"What's the towel for?" Julia couldn't help but ask.

Marley shrugged, "No clue. Lots of people have cleanliness issues, maybe he prefers to sleep on clean sheets after you guys play."

"It's hard to be in the mood when I don't know what's coming." Julia said with a groan as she took her place on the towel.

"Yeah, I can understand that, but think of it this way. This Top just paid a fortune for one night in your bed, and he wants it to be special or he wouldn't have given me strict instructions for you."

She knew the other woman was right, but Julia still had to beat back the urge to refuse when Marley began looping straps around her wrists and ankles. The straps were attached to the bedframe, and kept her limbs spread completely so that anyone walking into the room would get an eyeful of her pink pussy.

"Okay, one last thing," Marley said, holding up a satin blindfold.

"Is that really necessary?" Julia asked, getting a stern frown from the other sub.

"I don't know why you're fighting this. You've had at least six months of training. I came into this lifestyle a naïve idiot and threw myself on Lex's mercy."

Julia snorted in disbelief. "I've seen you two together. You're a match made in heaven."

"Or hell, whichever suits." Marley said with a laugh as she lifted Julia's pretty mask away and carefully placed it on top of her folded clothes. The satin blindfold replaced the lacy mask, and warmed quickly once it hit her skin, but she still shivered at the sensation of being in the dark. "Now, you have to stay put, blindfolded and quiet until he comes to you. When he does, you're under strict voice restriction; no speaking unless he asks you a direct question." Julia couldn't see Marley's eyes, but she could feel a gentle pat on her extended arm. "And don't be nervous. I have a feeling this guy is just a bit shy about his interest in you. I'm sure you'll get along nicely."

With that, Julia found herself tied naked to a bed in complete and utter silence. It was more nerve-wracking to lay there in the dark, anticipating what was to come, than it was standing on stage in front of everyone. In this position she couldn't resist. The guy who'd purchased her, had full license to use her as he wanted. That should have left her trembling in fear, but instead, she could feel her pussy clench at the thought of being taken and used. Would he start with foreplay, or just shove his cock into her as if she were a blow-up toy for his pleasure? What if she needed to say her safeword? She knew she couldn't get punished for safewording, but she was concerned about a man who would play before discussing it either way. Should she beg off? What would Killian tell her to do?

According to Lex, Killian had vetted the man, which meant he trusted him with a new sub. That had to count for something. Instead of questioning a man she didn't even know yet, she should just jump off the cliff and hope for the best. Resolved to wait patiently for her Master-for-the-night, she began reciting nursery rhymes in her head.

Mary, Mary quite contrary, how does your garden grow?

It seemed like hours before she heard the bedroom door open and the sound of heavy footsteps. There was no way to recognize the man's footsteps on the plush carpet, but she caught a whiff of a familiar cologne that tickled her brain. Whoever he was, she'd met him before, she just couldn't figure out where.

His steps stopped at the foot of the bed, and she was hyperaware of the fact that he was staring down at her naked form with a perfect view of her cunt. Did he like what he saw? She knew she was considered overweight in the outside world, but here, in this environment, she'd received such acceptance that it was easy to forget. Suddenly, her curves felt too round and her body too wide. She jolted in her bindings, instinctively trying to close her spread legs. A large hand covered her ankle, and began to stroke her gently.

The contact was enough to help her calm the surprise panic attack, and she inhaled sharply trying to clear her brain of all of her self-conscious thoughts. He wouldn't have purchased her if he didn't find her attractive. It wouldn't have made any sense. Firm in the knowledge that the man with the large hands had to want her, she let her body relax and focused on the warmth of his fingers sliding up the side of her calf.

He didn't hurry, and he didn't speak. He just kept touching her. First her ankle, then her calf, then up to her knee, where he took a moment to explore the sensitive crease at the back. She tried not to wiggle at the ticklish sensation, but her muscles twitched against his fingertips. He let out a small chuckle, and she tensed again.

The sound was so familiar. She'd heard it before. Now she was absolutely sure it was someone she'd interacted with, but who? Random people's face's populated her brain. From the regulars to the more recent additions, but no one seemed to fit.

When Ashton's face filled her mind's eye, she hesitated, and then shrugged it away. He was too experienced for the likes of her, and besides, she'd only seen him play with one-night subs, women who didn't want a regular Top to take care of them. The whole idea of the auction was to pair off unclaimed bottoms with suitable Tops. There was no way Ashton Reid would have wanted to jump into that pool, especially seeing as how he was the auctioneer.

Unable to pinpoint who her seducer was, she once again focused on his hand drawing lazy figure eights on her thigh, slowly but steadily making its way higher. She could feel her own juices leaking from her slit, and the fact that he could see it only made her hotter. There could be no doubt he was turning her on, and so far, he'd done nothing but touch her.

Just when he reached the crease between her thigh and her pussy, he stopped and pulled his hand away, making her whimper in disappointment. Another chuckle. Another familiar sound tickling her brain. Who was he?

A moment later she heard the sound of a zipper and the rustle of fabric. She assumed he was stripping, but with her eyes covered, she had no way of confirming it. When something warm and wet suddenly dripped onto her belly, she let out a shriek of surprise. For a moment, she thought he was jerking off on her stomach, and then he began massaging the moisture into her skin. It was oil of some kind. Massage oil, or coconut oil, perhaps? Both were popular at the parties. There wasn't much of a scent so she assumed it was the latter.

From hip–to-hip, and mound-to-throat, he firmly rubbed the oil all over her skin, leaving no spot untouched. By the time he finished, her nipples were hard, and her breasts were aching. She wasn't used to this kind of play. While they'd explored blindfolds and bondage, the classes focused more heavily on impact play and submission than sensual touch. Was she supposed to show her enjoyment, or just lie here?

Perplexed and horny, she shivered as the cool temperature of the bedroom combined with her now damp skin. Mr. Anonymous moved away from her, and she heard the buttons on a thermostat beep, before he returned. He'd turned the temperature up in the bedroom because he thought she was cold. Clearly, he was a caring Dominant. The knowledge helped her relax even further as he began rustling about, preparing whatever he had planned next.

A sharp pinch to her aching nipple made her gasp, and heat shot through her limbs. He twisted the nub harshly, and she felt her cheeks bloom with fire. He was testing her pain tolerance, and she felt her pussy respond instantly to the mix of pain and pleasure.

Chapter Six

Ashton's cock was so hard it was almost painful. Before he could start playing with her, he'd had to unzip his leathers to give it more room, or risk his zipper becoming permanently embedded in his shaft. Removing his shirt was simply for cleanliness. He would hate to get oil and wax all over it while he decorated his sub for the night.

Julia looked like an angel, spread-eagled on the bed, with her brilliant red hair fanned out around her like a halo, and her bare pussy on display. His mouth watered as the scent of her arousal filled the air around them, but he resisted touching her dampness. That was for later. Right now, he wanted her relaxed and as turned on as humanly possible. Perhaps on the verge of subspace even.

Surveying her for discomfort he took a moment to check her bindings. He didn't want them so tight they were cutting off the blood flow, but if they were too loose she might react and hurt herself. He wasn't going to take any chances when using hot wax in play.

Collecting the crock pot from the bathroom where he'd plugged it in earlier to heat the wax, he carried it to the bedside table and plugged it back in. The jars clinked slightly, and he froze, his gaze going to Julia on the bed. Did she recognize the sound?

When she didn't react, he breathed a sigh of relief, and moved on to slip a new vibrator from its package, quickly filling it with batteries. A feather, a comb, and a small bucket of ice completed his preparations, and he went back to her side.

Her full lips were parted, and her cheeks were pink with desire. She looked as beautiful as he imagined she would, and he began to second-guess his decision. What if she was angry at him when she realized he'd set this up? Did he really care what she thought? The fact that he was even questioning himself assured him that he did, but it was too late to change his decision now. Full steam ahead, consequences be damned.

Squeezing her lush breasts firmly, he marveled at the way they overflowed his palm. He had big hands, but she had glorious tits. It was one of the first things he'd noticed about her, and he wasn't ashamed to admit it. The second thing that had caught his attention was her full ass. It was perfectly shaped to take a pounding, and he'd seen it turn deliciously pink under a paddle and a flogger. He didn't have a spanking scene planned for tonight because he wanted to indulge them both with the wax, but if all went well, they'd be exploring her ass by dawn.

Settling himself on the bed next to her, he reached for the feather, and began dancing it over her skin. Instantly goosebumps rose on the pale pink flesh, and he saw her pulse jump in her throat. She tugged slightly on her bindings before relaxing again, but she didn't make a sound. The longer he teased her with the soft bristles of the feather, the harder she panted, and the tighter her muscles got.

With the flat of his hand he slapped the top of her bare mound, enjoying the sound of skin on skin. She jumped, and bit her bottom lip, but didn't make any noise. Stroking the feather of the now stinging skin of her pussy, he teased it down her slit, and then slapped her swollen clit.

This time, she arched up off the bed instinctively, before reining in her movement and tensing again.

She was fighting the urge to move. Had she mistaken his instructions for no conversation to mean no sounds and no movements as well? Feeling a bit irritated, he cupped Julia's cheek, and ran his thumb over her bottom lip. Her tongue followed his path, and he grinned down at her. She was definitely turned on. Maybe the misunderstanding was actually ramping up her desire. She was fighting her own instincts to please him, and that made his heart soar.

Determined to give her the night of her life, he reached for one of his jars, and tipped it slightly so that it dripped onto his wrist. The temperature was perfect. The heat blossomed over his skin, and his anticipation grew. She'd know the minute the wax hit her fair skin, or at least he assumed she would. He was the only Master she'd done wax play with that he knew of.

Immediately, a seed of doubt took root in his brain and he sat for a moment just staring at the blindfolded beauty on the bed. What if she'd played outside of the Lusty Fantasies group without anyone's knowledge? She might be far more experienced than he thought. For a moment, anger clouded his vision. The idea of a stranger touching her intimately made him want to vomit and break things at the same time.

She must have heard the change in the rhythm of his breathing, or sensed the tensing of his body, because suddenly, lines of worry bracketed her mouth. As he watched, she opened her lips, as though to speak, and then just as quickly clamped them shut again. She was good at following directions. A smug smile curled his lips, and he shook his head.

It didn't matter who she might have played with in the past. All that mattered was that for tonight she was his. He'd admired her from afar, but never considered actually taking her. There were just so many variables and what-ifs that he'd avoided the drama of a new sub, but now he instead of feeling dread, he felt a profound sense of hope. Maybe Julia was the woman he'd been looking for. She was certainly intelligent enough, and she oozed class even when she was on her knees in a submissive pose. He loved that about her.

"Are you still there?" she whispered, drawing him out of his thoughts. Her question was silly considering she could feel him next to her, and hear his breathing, but he'd been silent long enough that he figured she just needed reassurance he wasn't backing out. As tempted as he was to punish her for breaking his rules, he decided to follow his first instinct, and seduce her instead.

Placing his palm flat on her belly, he held it there, and murmured back, "Shh, of course I'm here, little one."

She inhaled sharply, and his name was on her exhale.

She knew.

He'd given himself away by speaking.

"No more speaking. Relax." He said firmly, ignoring the confused tension on her face. They could talk later, but first, he needed to show her without words how it might be between them.

Rubbing the coconut oil on her belly to make sure her skin still had a nice coating, he tipped the first jar of wax, and watched as the soft pink-colored liquid dripped onto the curve of her rib cage. Pink polka dots had never looked so sexy.

Her reaction was intense. Too intense for it to be just because of the wax. Instantly, his eyes were taking in every measure of her body. From the way her fingers were furled into fists, to the way her toes were pointed. Moisture still coated her plump pussy, but he wasn't willing to chance her not being into this. Sliding his empty hand down, he pushed it between the folds of her labia, and slid one finger into her tight passage before tipping the jar again, and dropping wax onto her hip this time. She clenched perfectly squeezing his finger in a death drip that would feel like fucking heaven on his cock.

Unable to hold back a groan, he gave her a small thrust of his hand so that his thumb was angled against her swollen clit. She moved once, twice, and then held still, her training kicking in. Pleased, he continued to drip hot wax from above until she looked like she'd been in a paint ball fight.

When he pulled away from her to put the jar of pink wax back in the pot, and pick another, she let out a soft moan of disappointment that thrilled him to no end. She knew who he was now, and she wanted him. The only thing better than the honest submission of a woman, was a woman's desire, and he had both.

~ ~ ~

Julia was lost in a haze of arousal. Ashton Reid had purchased her for the night, and it was his touch that was setting her on fire. How was that even possible? He hadn't given her any hint that he was interested since that one demonstration, and that had been nowhere near as intimate as this was already.

Just the feeling of his fingers in her cunt, made her want to beg for more, and it was nearly impossible to resist thrusting her clit against his thick thumb. She'd barely managed to contain the begging that was going on in her head as he slowly decorated her torso with hot wax. It felt like she had a coating over her whole abdomen, but she knew that was unlikely. Ashton liked to create works of art with his wax. He was meticulous in where and how he placed it. Each dot or line connected to another, and built the desire in his play partner.

If only she could figure out a way to relay how high her desire for him already was. When he pulled away, and cold air hit her wet pussy, she couldn't stop a moan of dismay. The sound filled her own ears and she cringed. Would he punish her this time? She'd broken his no sounds rule twice now.

His chuckle eased her concern, and she sighed with relief. She'd seen him as a playboy at the parties and as a hard-ass Dom with lethal focus during their demonstration, but this was the first time she'd felt seduced by him completely.

"Easy little one, I'm not finished painting your portrait yet." His voice sent lovely vibrations through her, and she held the sound in her head for as long as she could. Like the hot wax, it coated her soul, warming her and intensifying her feelings for him.

Content to be his canvas, she stretched her fingers, opening the fists that had been clamped shut since they'd been secured. A little painful wiggle, and then she sighed with relief.

"Good girl."

His words confirmed that he'd noticed the move, and assured her that he was still pleased with her. In her head she wondered at the man that laughed and played so easily in one setting, and then turned into this rake that held her captivated in his palm in another.

She was so lost in her own thoughts that she didn't register when he eased back into place until a dollop of wax hit the aching tip of her breast. A strangled sob broke from her throat, and she almost snorted trying to cut off the sound.

"Don't hold that back, Julia. I want to hear your pleasure now that you know who's touching you. I lift the voice restrictions."

Instantly, she felt more secure. Being able to speak gave her a sense of control back, and she opened her mouth only to feel him cover it with his own.

It was their first kiss, and it was monumental. Just the taste of him drew her deeper into his web, and she exchanged a sigh of pleasure with him before their tongues tangled. He was one hell of a good kisser, and she felt a flush building in her body as she responded down to her core. His free hand resumed its place between her thighs, but this time, he pinched her clit before shoving two fingers deep into her passage.

With a whimper of need, she broke their kiss and turned her head, enjoying the way his lips felt as they traveled over her jaw and down to the pulse in her throat. Sucking on the sensitive skin in time with his thrusting fingers, he brought her to the top of the mountain, and then demanded, "Come for me, now."

Explosions racked her body, and she felt her back arch up violently as she writhed on the bed. They'd barely begun to play, and she was already feeling sensations more intense than she'd ever experienced in her life. Her climax washed over her, draining her energy, and easing every tense muscle she might have had. When she was completely limp, he lifted away, and before she could react, he dropped more hot wax onto the likely bruised skin he'd just been suckling.

A gasp left her as her body rippled again, and she tossed her head on the pillow. Again, he dripped the wax, and again she wriggled under his ministrations. Over and over, the dance continued until she wondered at his control. She desperately wanted him to fuck her hard and deep, claiming her body.

As if she'd said the words out loud, she heard him groan with his own desire, and move away from her completely for a moment. The clink of jars and the shuffling of supplies was her only clue that he'd finished teasing her with the hot wax, but her hopes that he'd be sinking his cock into her were dashed when she felt the rake of something sharp on her hip.

Unable to control her own reaction, she flinched away from the implied danger, and tensed. He didn't say a word, but one of his hands landed firmly on her thigh, stinging the skin, and holding her in place. It was clear that she was meant to hold still while he proceeded with his plan.

The object scratched across her skin, sending shivers up her spine as it pulled the now cooled wax away and teased her sensitive flesh. The combination of sensations drove her crazy, and she heard herself whisper, "Please, Sir, I can't!"

"You can, Julia. Just take nice even breaths. In and out, that's it, good girl." His tone soothed her again like a good shot of aged whiskey, and she found herself relaxing in spite of the rioting sensations in her body. "I've dreamed of seeing you like this in my imagination, your sexy body covered in the wax just waiting for me to peel away the mask."

She was panting now, as his scraping tool made its way up over her ribcage, circling her breast, but avoiding the aching tip. Slowly but surely, he removed the wax from her body, scratching it away one layer at time. The object he used was sharp against her skin, but she knew he wouldn't hurt her, so she let herself bask in it. She wasn't sure if it was the focused attention he was giving every inch of her body, or the blade against her skin, but she was totally enamored with what he was doing.

"Your skin is a rosy pink color," he murmured. "It matches your pretty, pink pussy." Her thighs twitched at the thought of him staring at her most intimate folds, and he chuckled. "You can't hide it from me, love. I don't think you really want to, either. I think you've wanted this for as long as I have." He paused, and Julia held her breath. "Tell me, little one. Tell me you want this."

"I want this, Ashton. So much." The words tumbled off her tongue and emotion clogged her throat. She could feel tears dampen the blindfold, and she wondered why in the world he affected her so deeply. Maybe it was because he was the first Dominant she felt emotionally connected to, but maybe, just maybe, it was something more.

"Thank God," he growled, dropping whatever he'd been using to remove wax from her skin onto the bed beside her, and shifting his body between her spread legs. Anticipation made her tremble, as she felt the leather of his pants against her thighs and heard the rustle of a condom wrapper. "I had a lot more planned, but I have to be inside you right now. I'll make this up to you, love. I promise."

With that, he let his weight sink onto her, and she felt the bulbous head of his cock against her labia. She tipped her hips in welcome, and cried out with pleasure as he thrust his dick balls-deep into her clamping pussy.

~ ~ ~

He was in heaven. Julia's pussy felt like heaven on Earth, and if he died at this very moment, he'd go as a happy man. Just the way she gripped him with her internal muscles made him gasp for air and struggle to maintain his control. It took everything he had to hold still for thirty seconds and let her body adjust to his girth. Underneath him, she shuddered and squirmed for action, but the Dom in him wouldn't let her direct the show.

Resting on his knees between her open thighs, he was at an awkward angle, so he snagged a pillow and shoved it under her hips to lift her. The move lifted his cock up so that he was able to press against her g-spot with every thrust, and she squealed with pleasure.

Pinching her nipple hard, he slammed into her, grinding against her clit as he made contact.

"Oh, God!" she gasped, her head tossing. "Oh, my God!"

Another thrust brought more cries of pleasure, but by the fourth and fifth she was pleading with him for an orgasm again. Satisfied that they'd be coming together he reached down and pinched her clit, sending her into climax with an ear-shattering scream.

The death grip her cunt had on his cock sucked the cum right out of his balls, and he jerked with his own release, shouting out her name as he filled the condom near to bursting.

Chapter Seven

As she drifted back down to earth, Julia considered all of the possible ways she could react when she took the blindfold off. She could be angry that Ashton hadn't been honest with her in the beginning. She could be hurt that he'd felt the need to hide behind the blindfold. Or she could be understanding and hope that the feeling of intimacy they'd just experienced was as good for him as it was for her.

Neither of them moved for a long while, and although she enjoyed the weight of him sprawled across her, her body was growing numb.

"Master Ashton?" she murmured softly, feeling him lift his head to look at her. "I need to clean up."

"Of course." He moved away from her and the cool air of the room hit her sweat-slicked skin making her shiver. "After you finish we'll shower before we talk."

His hands made quick work of the bindings on her wrists and ankles, but he left her blindfold on. She felt his hand on her elbow helping her sit up, and she stayed that way for a moment. The idea of taking away the one last layer of protection scared the hell out of her. Once the satiny blindfold was gone, she was face to face with reality.

Her eyes were closed as she pulled the fabric away from her eyes. She opened them slowly, to find Ashton kneeling before her with concern on his face. "Do you need me to carry you, love?"

Unable to resist the big bad wolf turned prince charming, she giggled. "No, I'm sure I can walk. Thank you, Sir."

"Ashton. The scene is over, Julia. You can go back to calling me Ashton."

Trying to hide her hurt feelings, she nodded, "Does that mean we're through for the night then?"

"Not even close. Why would you think that?"

"Well, I mean, if the scene's over—"

"I have another ten hours with you. There's no way we're through yet. Hell, I want nothing more than to Top you for days. Just the thought of you tied up and waiting for me has me hard again." He tipped her chin up with one fingertip, and his silvery gray eyes met hers.

"I wanted you to have a few moments to collect yourself considering you went into this blind. I didn't want to scare you off, little bunny."

Wrinkling her nose at the term, she shook her head. "I'm not scared. A little confused, but not scared. Why all of the secrecy?"

Ashton's eyes crinkled at the corners as he grinned. "Would you believe I wanted to be mysterious?"

Arching one eyebrow, she shook her head.

"Okay, the truth is I didn't know I wanted to bid at all until tonight. Killian asked me to be the auctioneer in his stead; I saw your name on the list, and I guess I just got a wild hair. You seemed into the scene we did before, and I'm always looking for a sub who appreciates my particular kink."

Julia's heart clenched. Here she'd been hoping that it was all a dramatic ploy to win her heart, or at least collar her. What a naïve idiot she was. "So it was just an excuse to play with wax?"

Ashton gave her a strange look and then said, "It seemed like a good idea at the time, and you didn't safeword."

"Do you even know my safeword?" she snapped letting her hurt feelings overcome her better judgment. "With your no-speaking rule and the bindings, I just assumed there was no option for safewording."

His gray eyes darkened into finely honed granite and his jaw clenched. "You can always safeword if you need to. You know that. And I read your paperwork. Your safeword is Melody because it's your mother's name."

Flinching, she crossed her arms over her bare breasts and dropped her eyes away from his. "You could have just asked."

He pushed himself to his feet and reached for her hand, tugging her up from the bed. "That would have killed my anonymity. As it is, you figured me out the moment I spoke. Come on, let's get you cleaned up."

She tried to take a step and her knees buckled. The ground came rushing up toward her, but she was caught in mid-air by one strong arm. Ashton held her there as if her ample body weighed nothing, and she turned her head to look over her shoulder at him.

"Thanks."

"You're safe with me, Julia."

His words were a pointed reminder, and she thought it best not to respond. Instead, she let him help her steady herself on her feet, and follow her to the bathroom. Before she shut the door, she took one last look at him through the opening, admiring his lean, muscular physique. Standing there barefoot in just a pair of black leather pants, he looked like a dashing rogue sent to defile young virgins.

She giggled at the image once the door was shut when she realized that's pretty much exactly what he'd done. She was a virgin in the BDSM sense no more though. Now she'd be accepted as a full-fledged member of the community. She could have a partner in truth instead of just participating in demonstrations.

Never mind the fact that the only man she could see when she imagined her dream Master was patiently waiting for her to come out of the bathroom. Taking care of her business, she took a look in the mirror, and was surprised at her own appearance.

Her red hair was messy from tossing her head, and her green eyes seemed darker than normal. Here and there, colored wax still dotted her pink skin. She could see darker red marks on her thighs where Ashton had fucked her so hard, and a purplish bruise marred her throat. A hickey. Hell, she hadn't had a hickey since junior high.

The whole situation seemed utterly ridiculous. She was a grown woman with a hickey and a crush.

A knock on the door gave her just enough time to turn away from the mirror before Ashton poked his head through.

"Are you laughing?" he asked with a frown.

A giggle slipped from her lips and she nodded. "Yes, actually, I am." She pointed at her throat. "I haven't had one of these since JT Ward gave me one when I wouldn't let him get to second base at the Halloween party in seventh grade."

He looked at the bruise thoughtfully. "I should have made it darker. I like seeing my mark on you."

A flutter of pleasure rippled through her, and she stopped laughing. "You shouldn't say things like that Ashton."

"Why not? Are you offended by the truth?"

"No, but I'd rather not confuse things more than they already are."

"So I shouldn't tell you how hot you look with wax streaks on your perfect tits, and rings of canvas wear on your wrists?" he asked with a wicked glint in his eyes. She felt her mouth fall open in surprise, but no words came out. "Okay, then. I also won't tell you how fantastic your cunt feels wrapped around my cock, or how I'm planning on repeating the events from earlier at least a half dozen more times before noon."

She didn't remember him moving, but somehow he was standing right in front of her, the heat from his body seeping into hers. She stared up into his grey eyes with a mix of apprehension and excitement coursing through her veins.

"Half a dozen?" she questioned softly. "Sounds like high hopes to me."

He gave a half shrug, "I'm an optimist."

Without warning, he gripped her firmly by the hips and seated her on the counter between the two sinks. Stepping between her thighs, he pressed her back against the cold mirror just before he took control of her mouth with his. This time, it felt different, less strategic, and more impulsive—almost desperate. He dominated the kiss, sucking the fight right out of her. By the time he broke the kiss, desire had overwhelmed her good intentions, and she was ready to beg for more.

"Touch me, little one," he said as his hands slid around her body to cup her breasts, lifting them to his mouth. He didn't seem put off by the fact that oil still glistened on her skin as he sucked one plump nipple into his mouth and teased it with his teeth.

Taking him at his word, she gave herself the freedom to explore the parts of him she could reach. She loved the strong line of his shoulders and the ripples of muscles down his back, but it was his chest and abs that made her wet with need. Nudging him upward, she had to bite back a groan when he released her nipple with a sucking pop and lifted his head so that she could reach his torso.

Like a golden Adonis, he was toned in all the right places, with a firm body that she envied and admired. Ridges of muscle roped his abdomen when he moved, reminding her of the term washboard abs. If anyone fit that phrase it was Ashton Reid. He was completely hairless until just below his belly button, and she followed that trail of dark blonde hair to the top of his leather pants. Bravely she ran her finger along the top edge of his pants, skimming the sensitive skin and peering up at him coyly.

"Master Ashton, can I open your leathers?"

She saw a flicker of something new in his eyes, and then like donning a mask, his face reverted back to that of the Dom she was so familiar with. There was no more of the teasing, playful flirt left from before.

"Do it." The words were a harsh command, but they sounded perfect to her ears, and she was quick to follow the instruction.

Releasing the snap on his leathers, she eased the zipper down carefully so as not to catch him in it. His long, hard cock popped free, and she heard herself gasp. "Holy shit."

An arrogant grin broke over his face, and he cocked his head. "What's the matter, little one? Don't tell me you're scared now. You took him like a champ earlier."

"I can't believe you didn't rip me in two," she declared, firmly wrapping her hand around the bobbing member. Her fingertips just barely touched, but it was the length that was really impressive.

"You were ready for me." The statement rang with more truth than he could have realized, but she didn't reply back. Her brain was going haywire imagining him pushing that beautiful cock inside of her again.

Spreading her thighs, she tugged him forward just a bit, and then stopped and looked to him for direction. He was watching her like a hawk, and the moment she stopped, he took over. Lining his cock up with her open pussy, he rubbed the bulbous head through her moisture making her hiss.

"What was that about half a dozen being too optimistic?" He asked, just before he pressed into her waiting body.

She cocked her hips to make room for his length and shoved her fingers into his hair, gripping and tugging a little. She was unsure what to do with her hands now that she was unbound. Some Doms hated a sub touching them affectionately, but he'd asked her to touch him before. How would he feel while they were fucking?

Tentatively, she put one hand on his chest, and gave his pec a firm squeeze. When he didn't resist, she slid it up to his shoulder, and added the other hand to the back of his neck. The movement drew them closer and his thrusting cock sank even deeper making her eyes roll back in her head. Holy hell, he touched her everywhere.

With a solid grip on him, she held on and just enjoyed the ride as he pounded into her flesh. His mouth came down on her shoulder, and she let out a cry of pleasure when he nipped the skin. A moment later, she realized that her ass no longer rested on the vanity top, and his hands were spreading her cheeks wide as he held her.

With every thrust his large balls swung forward, brushing against her asshole, and that combined with his pelvic bone slamming into her clit was enough to make her dizzy. Holding him tighter, she pressed her breasts firmly against his chest.

"Fuck yeah, you feel like a glove on my cock." He growled into her ear. "I could stay here for the rest of my days."

She tried not to read more into the words, but it was hard to resist. They seemed to fit together so perfectly, and her craving for him was intense. What would he say if she came out and asked him to collar her? He'd likely laugh in her face.

Ashton instantly seemed to notice her distraction, because he lifted his head and stopped moving. "What's wrong? Are you hurt?"

She shook her head, "I'm perfect, Sir. Don't stop."

Doubt registered on his face, and he pulled back even farther, easing her butt back onto the counter. Disappointed and embarrassed, Julia felt her cheeks warm. This was it; he was going to walk away now.

"Turn around, love."

The words caught her off guard, and she stayed put staring up at him in confusion.

"Turn your pretty ass around, sub."

Shivering at the intensity in his words, she moved quickly to comply, turning her body to face the mirror. He pushed her down, bending her over the vanity and resumed his position between her thighs. Shoving his cock back into her body, he ran his hands over her upturned ass cheeks.

"You've got a beautiful ass, subbie." He split her wide, and stroked his thumb over her anus, making her clench down on his cock. "I seem to recall your checklist mentioned you liked anal."

It wasn't a question, so she stayed silent, but if she'd been able to respond she'd have told him how much she enjoyed anal. She pressed back on his thumb so that just the tip dipped into her tight backside.

"Perfect."

That one word was the only warning she got before he pushed his finger into her ass, stretching her until he could add a second and then a third. With only her own juices as lube, the movement burned some, but she absorbed the pain letting it become part of her desire. There was something deliciously taboo about letting a man take her ass.

Ashton continued fucking her pussy with his cock while preparing her ass for several minutes, and just when she was on the verge of coming he pulled his fingers and cock completely away from her.

"No coming, little one." He admonished, bending over her back, and gripping her tits tightly. "You're greedy for an orgasm aren't you?"

He manipulated her breasts harshly, pinching and pulling at the mounds until she was squirming under him. She'd likely have bruises tomorrow, but damn, his hands were magic on her skin.

"Julia, look at me."

She hadn't even realized her eyes were shut until he spoke, but when she forced them open and met his gaze in the mirror, she was shocked at their reflection. His blonde hair was a stark contrast to her wicked, red mane, and she looked wild with her eye makeup smudged and her lips swollen. He held her around the middle with his hands lifting her double E cup breasts so that they looked gloriously full, and she felt like an erotic goddess.

"I'm going to fuck your ass, little one. What's your safe word?"

Immediately she realized that he was attempting to gauge her mindset, and she mumbled out the words, "Melody, Sir."

"Good girl. Put your face on the counter." He helped press her into the position he wanted her, with her cheek and arms on the marble countertop, and her ass up in the air. She heard him open the cabinet beside her, and she assumed he was looking for something to use as lube.

Still, she was unprepared for the icy cold goop that hit her asshole a moment later. He was quick to spread the gel, and before long, his fingers were sliding in and out of her backside with ease.

The first push forward with his cock still took her breath away. He was bigger than she'd ever taken anally, but that didn't mean she was going to stop him. She wanted it too much.

"Fucking hell, you're tight," he growled, his hands once again gripping her ass and spreading her wide. She helped by inching her feet further apart and bearing down to relax her ass around him. When he finally breached the two tight rings of muscle, they both let out a sigh of relief, and she clenched her eyes closed to focus on the sensation.

Carefully, he moved in and out of her in short thrusts until her body adjusted to his invasion. The moment she felt his pubic hair brush against her ass cheeks, she gave herself a silent cheer. It was hard to believe all of him fit, but damn, he did feel good.

Once they had the fit right, Ashton was able to move freely, and Julia encouraged his thrusts by rocking backwards to meet him. The harsh motion chaffed her breasts, which were rubbing against the stone countertop, but it didn't slow her down. When she moved her hand back to her own hip, he grabbed it, and reached for the other. Holding her wrists together against her lower back, he now had her completely at his will. She couldn't have moved away if she'd wanted to, but no sane person would try to escape this pleasure.

"Do you like my cock, Ms. Sweet? How would all of those posh businessmen we deal with feel if they knew I'd had my cock up your ass? Maybe we'll have to demonstrate this at the next board meeting."

She could picture it in her head. Ashton bending her over the massive mahogany table in the boardroom at her office building, shoving the skirt of her suit up over her hips and sinking into her from behind as the eleven other board members watched and envied them.

The fantasy was too much, and she began to spasm as her orgasm hit her unexpectedly. Jerking upwards off the vanity, she stared at herself in the mirror, while Ashton continued to pound her ass. Her breasts bounced, and her mouth hung open on a silent cry of pleasure. When he shouted her name and filled her body with his cum, she screamed in return, absorbing a second climax almost immediately after the first. A complete wave of relaxation washed over her, and she didn't even notice when he lowered her back down to rest on the counter again.

Chapter Eight

He'd seen subs in subspace many times, but generally, it was after an intense scene. Julia had drifted off, and he couldn't ignore the feeling of pride in his chest as he lifted her and carried her over to the glass-enclosed shower. Stepping inside, he took a seat on the built-in bench, and settled her on his lap with her face tucked into his neck to protect it. The water came out cold at first, and he shielded her as much as he could until it warmed up. Then he leaned back and let it pour over them as he held her gently and murmured to her.

Part of him hoped she could hear and understand his whispered words, and part of him was scared that if she could, she'd panic and run. He didn't completely understand why he felt so deeply for this woman, but the connection was impossible to deny. He couldn't remember the last time he'd come so hard twice in a row with the same woman, and if it weren't for the fact that she was in a daze, he'd most likely be hard for her again.

It was time to face facts. The respect he'd always had for her as a businesswoman, paled in comparison to the desire he felt for her as a submissive. He hadn't purchased her for one night of play. He'd purchased her because he couldn't tolerate the thought of another Dom touching her. Now that he'd been inside of her delicious body, that possessiveness was only going to get worse.

What if she didn't feel the same way? She was a neophyte after all. She'd barely dipped her toes into the world of BDSM, and here he was dreaming about collaring her and keeping her to himself. What if she wanted to explore other things and other people before settling into a serious relationship?

The last two words gave him pause. The last serious relationship he'd had had been almost ten years ago. Since then, he'd only played with submissives on a temporary basis. The idea of being tied to one and responsible for her hadn't appealed to him. Until now.

Julia moaned and shifted in his arms. Her eyes were still pretty hazy, but she looked adorable—all sex-tousled and wet from the shower.

"Welcome back," he said. "That was one of the best orgasms I've ever had."

He refused to consider what his words implied, and then decided he didn't really care about the implications. She moved him in a way he'd never experienced before. He admired and respected her as a person, and he desired her as a woman. She was submissive, but with just enough brat in her to push back when she felt uncomfortable, and he appreciated that. If he could choose anyone to wear his collar, he'd pick her.

"Ditto," she murmured. She remained in his arms for several more minutes, the water keeping them comfortably warm, before she seemed to find her bearings again. "I need to wash up, but I'm not sure I can stand yet."

He nodded his understanding, and reached for the clean cloth that hung on a bar near his head. Expensive bath products lined a shelf set in the wall, and he added some shower gel to the cloth while being careful not to juggle her around too much. When he began to wash her gently, she frowned up at him.

"I can do that."

With a laugh he shook his head, "I don't think so. This is my favorite part of aftercare. This is when you're all soft and sexy and I get to explore your beautiful curves."

A pink blush stole up her cheeks and he wondered at a woman who could take a cock in her ass one minute and blush at being bathed the next.

"I haven't had anyone bathe me since I was a child," she confessed, watching his hand move up and down her legs, washing every inch of her. He paused, considering her words and how he should respond, and then moved his hand higher to her thighs.

"I'm pleased to be your first."

She lifted her eyes and met his. "You're also my first Top."

He nodded.

"I thought you didn't like new subs?"

Shrugging, he continued washing away the oil and stickiness from between her thighs. He worked as gently and efficiently as he could because he knew her clit was probably a bit tender. She was right, he didn't like new subs. He'd said so a dozen times, yet here he was.

"You're different."

"How?"

"You know, you're awfully chatty for a sub who just spent twenty minutes in subspace."

"I'm sorry, Sir. I didn't realize we were still in the scene." She dropped her head submissively and tensed in his arms again. He hated seeing her withdraw from him, but he didn't plan on his next words until they spilled from his mouth.

"I like you more than I should."

Her face lifted and her eyes were wide with surprise. Her red hair made her skin look extra pale against her brilliant green eyes. "You do?"

"Come on, I'll help you stand up so that we can wash the other side." He said, ignoring her curiosity. He didn't have the answers he was sure she was looking for, so it was best to just avoid saying anything else.

Helping her lean heavily against the tiled shower wall, he crouched behind her and ran the cloth up over her round backside and between her cheeks. She inhaled sharply when his cloth pressed against her used asshole, but otherwise, she remained quiet while he finished washing her body.

"Would you like me to wash your hair?" he murmured, kissing her just below her ear, and massaging the nape of her neck.

"No, thank you. If I use anything but my own shampoo it turns into a briar patch. It's one of the joys of artistically colored hair."

Her smile was small, but it was genuine, and he responded in kind. "I like your hair. It's eye catching."

She giggled, "It certainly is. I know it catches some of the men I deal with off guard. CEOs aren't supposed to have fire-engine-red hair with pink streaks."

"Pink streaks?"

"Oh yeah, they're in there. You probably didn't notice because of the lighting, but in the sunshine you can see them. I actually dyed it the first time the day I broke off my engagement to my ex. I wanted a new me."

"I didn't know you were engaged."

She shrugged but didn't explain, and he frowned down at her.

"Tell me Julia. I want to know more about you."

"We were kids, and neither of us really loved each other the way we should. I didn't know until I met Killian exactly what was missing in that relationship."

Ashton's heart stopped in his chest. "You dated Killian?"

Nodding, she closed her eyes and ducked her head under the water. When she came back out, he stepped under the shower and quickly washed without another word. He hadn't realized she'd dated his best friend and boss. Killian didn't date women he couldn't sleep with, so that meant he'd been inside Julia at one point in time. Jealousy and rage burned in his chest, and he fought to control it. He smacked the metal faucet harder than planned to shut the water off, and Julia jumped.

"Are you okay? Did I do something wrong?"

"I'm fine. The water's just getting cold." He turned away from her, and stepped out to grab towels. He quickly toweled himself off and wrapped it around his hips. He turned back just in time to see her cover her gorgeous full figure with the soft cotton towel, hiding it from view.

Her movements were sharp, and he realized she was confused by his sudden change in demeanor.

"You slept with Killian." He watched her for her reaction. It wasn't a question, or an accusation, but her chin tipped defiantly and her eyes flashed.

"And?"

"And I'm jealous."

Her mouth dropped open, and she stared at him in shock. "What?"

"I wasn't your first Top."

"Yes you were. Killian showed me a few things, but I didn't know what it meant when we were together. I might have always been submissive, but I didn't submit in the bedroom until I learned more. You *are* my first Dom, Ashton."

Just hearing those words, filled him with such a level of pride and pleasure that he grinned, and reached for her. Slamming her against his body, he cupped her ass and kissed her deeply. Tangling his tongue with hers, and nipping at her lips before he released her.

"Who's the better lover?" he asked playfully. When she blushed again and shook her head, he laughed, "I'm just teasing. I already know I'm better than K is. It wasn't him making you scream tonight."

"No, it wasn't," she agreed, arousal sparking in her eyes again.

~ ~ ~

Julia wasn't sure what to think about Ashton Reid at this point. He was like a bipolar schizophrenic tonight. Every time she spoke he seemed to shift gears, and it was making her head spin. What exactly did he want from her?

Leading the way back in to the bedroom, Ashton quickly stripped the cover off the bed, and pulled the blankets back for her to crawl in. She noted the supplies still on the bedside table, and her eyes landed on the comb in his hand.

"It was a comb?" she asked. When he looked down at it in confusion, she clarified. "It felt sharp like a knife, but I didn't think you were into knife play. Now I understand; it was a comb you were using to remove the wax."

He grinned and twirled the cheap plastic in his hand. "Yep, an old trick from the man who taught me. It increases the sensation of the wax removal, amplifying the intensity of the scene."

"It sure as hell does." She agreed. "So, what's the ice for?"

"That's another method for removing wax, but we'll get to it another time." He climbed into the bed next to her, and pulled her into his chest. "I like to cuddle after a scene."

"Most men hate to admit they like cuddling."

"I'm not most men."

"I'm not much of a cuddler," she grumbled.

"I've noticed that normally you don't like being touched. You certainly seemed to enjoy it when you're submitting it though."

She shrugged again, "I wasn't raised that way. My family wasn't affectionate. It feels awkward to have someone touch me when we're not having sex. It's not like I hate it; it's just weird. Tell me, how did you get into wax play?"

With her cheek on his chest she couldn't see his facial expression to know if she was overstepping, but she hoped that he liked pillow talk as much as he liked cuddling after sex.

"I told you during the demonstration."

"I was, uh, a bit distracted. I was your volunteer, remember?"

"So does that mean you weren't paying attention to my words then, subbie?" he said playfully, skimming his fingertips over her hip and making her shiver. "I've always had a fascination with fire and melted wax. When I was a kid, I used to use my mom's home party candles to make pictures on paper plates, and I would hurry to throw them away before I got caught. When I got into BDSM and realized there was such a thing as wax play, it was pretty much a given for me. I studied at a club in Texas because there's a Master there who specializes in fire and wax play. Louis is a genius. He's actually a fairly well known artist using fire to scorch metal and wood into artistic sculptures. That piece in Killian's office is one of his."

"The one of the mermaid?" Julia asked, visualizing the piece in her mind. She's seen it more than once, and it was a stunning image, but the fact that it had been done with fire blew her mind. "I always assumed that was painted.

"Nope, that's the genius behind it. What he does is astonishing. I'd love to take you up there to meet him and watch him work some time."

Julia wasn't sure what to say. The auction had been a one-night deal, but Ashton was acting like they might have a future of some sort. Unable to turn him down in the hopes that he really might see more for them, she nodded against his chest. "Sure, maybe some of the other subs would like to go, too."

"That's not exactly—well, anyway, I love the way wax melts into one fluid piece, but the colors never blend with each other. They stay separate while becoming something new. I think people need to practice that ability, and I try to implement this observation in how I run my business ventures."

Considering he was extremely successful in running the companies he did for Killian, she figured he was on to something.

"So, you're saying you're a good team builder?"

"I suppose in laymen's terms, yes. I think a team has to be well balanced with knowledge and creativity, but the pieces have to come together like a puzzle. If one piece doesn't fit right, the picture won't come together."

"Why don't you have businesses of your own, then? I mean, you still work for Killian, right?"

"Yep, and I probably always will. We've been friends since college, and if it weren't for him, I wouldn't have graduated with a degree. I was too focused on fucking and drinking back then." His laughter was contagious, and Julia enjoyed the feeling of his chest rumbling under her. He felt like a cozy teddy bear with rock-hard muscles, and she never realized how much she missed cuddling up with a teddy bear. Fidgeting a bit, her knee brushed against his cock, and she was surprised to find it was still semi-hard.

"Don't mind him." He pressed a kiss to the crown of her head, and she felt unusually warm under the affectionate gesture.

How was she supposed to keep from falling for him when he was being such a great guy? At this rate, she'd be heartbroken when they separated tomorrow. For a moment, she let herself consider the idea that they wouldn't separate, and he would ask her to wear his collar. It was a silly notion, but one that warmed her heart anyway.

Buoyed by the emotional thought, she murmured, "Actually, I was hoping to get a better view of him."

"Really, hmm…" He pushed the covers back, exposing his golden body to view, and she once again found herself drooling over his rock-hard muscles, and the delicious looking cock that rose to point her way. "Get closer if you want a good look."

His words were sharp, and echoed with desire, making her feel needy all over again. Some Doms didn't like it when a sub initiated a scene, but she went with her gut, scooting down the bed, smiling at him sweetly. "Master Ashton, may I suck your cock?"

"Fuck yes," he said, breathing deeply through his nose, so that his nostrils flared.

His grey eyes grew dark as she leaned over him to grab a piece of ice from the bucket before climbing between his legs. There was no way she'd be able to deep-throat him, but she'd still give him the blowjob of his life.

With the ice cold on her tongue, she quickly dipped her head and licked his cock, making him jerk in her hand. She grinned, and using the ice between her lips, she wet him generously. Once she'd gotten him all wet, she went to work with her hands, twisting gently but firmly as she slid them up and down his long cock. Moving her mouth back to his sensitive corona, she worked the nearly melted ice chunk against the soft skin with her teeth.

"Sonuvabitch you're good at that, woman," he hissed, his head tipping back and his eyes closing. His knees rose on either side of her, and he began to thrust up into her mouth, hitting the back of her throat with each push.

She gagged a bit, and spittle slid down his length making him even wetter. He groaned and pumped harder, until she had to pull away to catch her breath. Looking up at him, she wrinkled her nose and kissed the head of his cock.

"Are you okay, little one?" Concern etched his face, even as desire filled his eyes.

"I'm great. I just have to remember to breathe on occasion," she replied with a quick wink before she took his cock back in her mouth. With the ice melted and gone now, she moved one hand down to cup his balls, while she continued the twisting stroke on his shaft with the other. Before long, she felt his balls tighten, and his upward thrusting started again.

"I'm gonna come, love, suck me dry," he growled, and she looked up through her lashes at him, making eye contact just as he shot his cum into her mouth. Swallowing as fast as she could, she barely managed to hold his gaze as cum dribbled from her lips and down his length. After a few moments, he began to soften, and she released him, licking her lips.

Chapter Nine

Ashton stared down at the sleeping woman in his arms and really looked at the fine details of her face. She had perfectly sculpted eyebrows and long eyelashes that formed perfect crescents on her high cheekbones. Her lips were a sexy pink color even though she wore no lipstick on them at this point. Even the smeared eye makeup didn't detract from the pale beauty of her skin, and he ran his fingertip over the soft jawline, enjoying the way she turned her head to him while she slept.

It was almost as if she knew instinctively she was safe in his arms, or at least he hoped that's what it meant. Julia Sweet was everything he'd ever wanted in a woman, and he held her in his arms. How was he going to make her want to stay there?

Years ago, he'd collared a sub, and it had been a disaster. Kimmie had been difficult and demanding from the get-go, but he was young, and he truly believed she could learn to be submissive. Now he knew better. He knew that he wanted a woman who was strong enough in herself to accept her own submissive needs. A woman like Julia.

The sound of a bell chiming in the hallway signaled the end of the party, and the call for brunch in the dining room, but he didn't want to wake her.

After several more minutes, a knock rattled the door and Doug called out, "Brunch call. Ten minutes."

The sound woke his sleeping beauty, and he let her roll away from him, still rubbing sleep from her eyes. She glanced at the clock and her eyes widened. "Wow. I can't believe I slept this late."

"We were up until dawn, little one. You didn't actually get that much sleep."

She frowned his way. "Did you sleep at all?"

He shrugged, "A bit. I'm not used to sleeping with someone."

"Sorry," A guilty expression crossed her face before she turned away, and he hurried to comfort her.

"I found it intriguing, and enlightening actually. I'd like to do it again."

Halfway out of the bed, she froze and sat stock still on the edge of the mattress. Without turning around, she said softly, "I'm glad you enjoyed it. Sleeping in someone's arms is very intimate. Too intimate for some."

"It used to be too much for me," He agreed, moving to kneel behind her. Moving her hair to the side, he kissed her shoulder. "Or, at least I hadn't found anyone I wanted to sleep with until now. Would you consider sleeping with me again?"

"Sleeping with you?" she questioned, and he laughed.

"Absolutely, scout's honor. If you come to my bed, I will let you sleep at some point."

Julia turned, and looked at him through narrowed eyes. When she realized he was teasing her, she laughed. "I thought you were serious for a minute."

"I am. There's something between us, Julia. Something good." He moved to stand in front of her, taking her hands in his. "Would you consider going on a date with me, Ms. Sweet?"

"Ashton, you don't have to do this—"

"I don't have to do anything I don't want to, but I want to do this. It's been years since a woman interested me in more than just a shallow way. I've known you as a businesswoman, a submissive, and hopefully, now, I will get to know you as a friend. With any luck, our friendship will grow into more, but I'll respect your wishes either way. Now, don't leave me hanging. Will you go out on a date with me?"

Julia stared up at him with wide eyes, but he couldn't discern the emotion behind them. For a moment he let himself consider the possibility that she would reject him, and his heart raced with anxiety.

"Yes. I'd like that," she finally murmured in response.

Overjoyed, he pulled her up from the bed, and wrapped his arms around her middle, lifting her and spinning them in a circle. "Thank God. For a moment I thought you were going to turn me down, subbie."

"We need to discuss a contract if I'm going to be in your bed though, Master Ashton," she reprimanded. Her voice sounded adorably stern, but her eyes were filled with pleasure. "I can't have you taking advantage of me. I'm still a newly-aware submissive, remember?"

"Hell no you're not. You're mine," he insisted, planting his mouth on hers, and laying claim to every part of her he could. Brunch be damned. He was going to make love to *his* woman.

Chapter Ten

"Did you tell the auctioned pairs specifically?" Killian asked Doug as he returned to the dining room alone.

"Of course I did. There was no answer from any of the bedrooms, and in several, there was active play happening inside." Doug smiled widely, taking his seat next to his wife.

Alana laughed, "Sounds like all of the subs auctioned off last night are happy with the results."

Killian smiled smugly, "Of course they are. I planned for all possible contingencies. The only one I had any concern about was Julia, and I believe the right man for the job stepped up."

Cocking her head curiously, Alana brushed her long blonde hair from her face, "I thought she was purchased by Lex and Marley?"

"Not exactly." Lex answered as he stepped into the room, Marley following behind. Marley's steps were careful, and it was obvious she was aching. Alana jumped to her feet to collect a bottle of ibuprofen and a cushion to sit on, passing both to the other woman.

"Lex was purchasing Julia for a friend, I believe." Killian speculated. He watched Lex settle his sub on a cushioned chair before taking a seat next to her.

"Yes, actually, and that friend is the one who spent the night with her. My Marley is enough for me." He lifted Marley's hand and kissed her palm before pouring her a glass of juice and filling her plate with food.

"So, who is it?" Alana asked.

When Lex didn't respond, she huffed with frustration. "You can't leave us hanging like that. Killian, who spent the night with Julia?"

"Ashton," he answered softly.

The room was quiet but for the clinking of silverware on plates, and Killian met Alana's gaze directly.

"Ashton? But he never takes a permanent sub. I thought the idea was to get the virgin subs paired off with responsible Tops? People they might have a future relationship with." Alana prodded. Killian gave her a hard look, silencing her questions before he spoke again.

"Ashton has never taken a permanent sub, but that doesn't mean he never will." With that, Killian went back to eating, letting the subject die. He never planned on explaining to anyone how he'd orchestrated the evening to hook his friend into a relationship. He'd known six months ago when he admitted Julia to the training program that Ashton would be perfect of her, and he was pleased to see his plans succeed.

"Good morning all!" Daniel announced as he entered the room, his arm wrapped tightly around Kitty's waist.

"Well you're more cheerful than normal this morning," Killian observed, his eyes taking in the other man's protective arm roped around his submissive.

"I certainly am! We have news to share," Daniel said excitedly, lifting Kitty's hand and kissing her knuckles.

"Before you tell us, how are you feeling this morning Kitty?" Killian interrupted, his eyes holding the petite woman in place. She blushed and looked up at Daniel for permission to speak.

"I'm wonderful, Master Killian, thank you."

Daniel quickly addressed the confusion in the room. "I'm not sure who knows that we had a bit of an issue last night while doing a scene, and Kitty spaced out more quickly than normal. At first I was concerned, but when she came to we began talking about what might have caused the intensity of her reaction. I'm overjoyed to announce that we're having a baby!"

Everyone gasped, and the congratulations rolled out as Daniel and Kitty beamed with joy. Killian felt something warm fall into place as he looked around the room. This group of friends had become a family of sorts. An unconventional one for sure, but they relied on each other for security, approval, and strength. He felt like a proud father, even though he had no children of his own.

"That's wonderful news. Congratulations to both of you." He lifted his coffee mug in a toast. "I assume you'll be taking a hiatus from our monthly events?"

Daniel nodded, but Kitty shook her head and laughed. "Women have been having babies since the beginning of time Master. I'm almost certain we can still attend the parties without harming our child."

Wrinkling his nose, Daniel frowned. "Yeah, okay, we'll still come occasionally, but only when she's feeling up to it. And not until the doctor gives me direct approval that it's safe. Killian, I owe you a debt I can never repay."

"Why is that?" Alana asked curiously.

"Killian brought Kitty to me. Initially, she was just going to assist me in demonstrations, but she stole my heart, and now...I can't believe it. I'm going to be a dad!" Daniel threw his fist up in the air as though he was cheering on his favorite sports team.

Laughter filled the room, echoing through the quiet house, and Killian joined in the playful discussion regarding Daniel's strict parenting plans. Somewhere on the floor above a scream of pleasure filled the air, and he had to hide another grin.

Perhaps he'd consider another auction for the Christmas party this year as he had another class graduating around them. The masquerade was over, and once all of the happy couples were revealed, no one would fall for that plot again. Brainstorming as he ate, Killian enjoyed the rest of his brunch with his submissives, and friends. All the while, plotting for the next pairing.

The End

Continue Reading for Watching Sin
Fetish & Fantasy Book 1

Watching Sin

A Fetish & Fantasy Novella

Lori King

Blurb

After fifteen years as a bland housewife, Alana is ready to shake up her life by fulfilling her darkest fantasy. She wants to be watched. Her exhibitionist streak is ready to break free, and she knows exactly whom she wants for her voyeur.

Doug would give his wife, Alana, the moon if she asked, so he's more than willing to participate in a public threesome at a fetish party if it makes her kinky wishes come true. His business partner and best friend, Killian is the wild card in their plan.

A businessman first, and a trained Dominant second, Killian never gets tied down to one submissive. He's a lover with commitment issues, but he doesn't hesitate to help fulfill Doug and Alana's fantasies. Once the fantasy is set in motion, the three players must decide if watching sin is enough...

Dedication

For the other Rebels.
It's a long road, but it's worth it.

Chapter One

Doug...

"Can we? Just this once, Doug, please?" Her voice was a husky moan in his ear, and he could deny her nothing.

For the last four months, they had attended the monthly Fetish parties as voyeurs only. He had watched with lust-filled eyes, as the people around them sought release for their passion, hoping that at some point his wife would grow comfortable enough with the parties to join in. But each time she maintained her distance, standing off to the side, watching the sweat-soaked strangers explore the bodies around them, her face devoid of emotion. He knew she felt something; her racing pulse and sharp intake of breath betrayed her stoic exterior, and by the time he got her home after each party, she was desperate for his cock.

Her voracious appetite for sex seemed to stem from her love of erotic romance novels. He regularly caught her with her nose in a book, cheeks flushed, eyes glassy, and pussy dripping. One of these days he would have to write a thank you letter to the publishers for keeping his cock in working form, but for tonight, he had other things to focus on.

Alana stood beside him, asking his permission to put on a show. She wanted him to strip her down, and fuck her in front of the other partygoers. His eyes met hers and he could see the fire burning in their sapphire-colored depths.

What had changed her mind? What had her so turned on tonight that she couldn't deny her own need anymore?

The brush of a hand over his shoulder drew his attention, and he instantly understood. The man standing at his elbow was his best friend and business partner, Killian Whitfield. In his black and white tuxedo he looked more like a Hollywood movie star walking the red carpet than a businessman still trying to crack the million-dollar mark.

"Doug, Alana. How are you both this evening? Enjoying the…festivities I hope."

Killian stood too close to Alana for propriety, yet Doug wasn't put off. He was surprised to find that he *wanted* to put on a show for his friend. If Alana was willing to fuck in front of Killian, what else would she be willing to do with him present? He felt his dick thicken a little at the image of his wife on her knees sucking Killian's cock in the middle of the living room. Never before had he fantasized about his wife with another man, but he could picture it with Killian. In his mind's eye, he could see his friend's long lean body, flexing and rippling with desire as his wife sucked him dry. That would be incredible to watch, and by the look on Alana's face, she could picture such an event too. What a surprise this evening was turning out to be.

"We're having a wonderful time. These parties are always memorable, Killian." As Alana spoke, her eyes drifted over Killian's six foot tall frame, and back up to meet his assessing green eyes. When their gazes collided, Doug could almost see sparks crackling in the air around them, and his cock hardened in his pants until he had to fidget to give his erection more room. He took the opportunity before it slipped away, and wrapped his arm around the curve of Alana's waist, drawing her even closer between the two men.

"Actually Killian, Alana was just commenting that she wanted to *enjoy* the party a little more tonight."

Doug watched Killian's eyes flame at the implication, and his own cock throbbed in response. Could he actually do this? Could he fuck Alana in front of these people? The answering electrical current pulsing through his body was the only confirmation he needed to know he absolutely could do that and more. Alana's heavy-lidded gaze was a potent aphrodisiac, but when paired with Killian's commanding masculinity, it made Doug dizzy with need.

Killian didn't hide his charisma or his flirty nature; he openly charmed both sexes. Doug had never seen him with another man, nor had he ever blatantly asked him if he was bisexual, but there were rumors. Everyone knew he was open to anything when it came to sex. Hell, how many times had they swapped stories while they waited to tee off on the golf course? Doug had no problem sharing the kinky things he and Alana liked to try in the privacy of their own home, and Killian encouraged him to give every salacious detail. Perhaps there was more to his interest than pure, perverted male curiosity.

"Really? Is there some way I could be of assistance in making all your desires come true, Alana?" Killian's silky smooth baritone voice rippled through Doug's chest, and he heard Alana's sharp intake of breath.

Her eyes darted to meet Doug's, and he smiled reassuringly at his wife. If they were going to do this, they were going in with their eyes open. "I believe she'd like you to watch to begin with."

Killian stepped a little closer to the two of them and lowered his voice, directing his next question to Alana, "I'll only ask this once, but I have to ask. Would you like to stay here, or go into one of the bedrooms where we have more privacy?"

The ultimate question in Doug's mind was whether or not she actually wanted to put on a show for the entire bevy of strangers in the room, or just for Killian. The air around them grew tense as Alana considered her first foray into exhibitionism.

"I believe I'd prefer to throw caution to the wind tonight. Will you help me?" she said softly as she stared up into Killian's face.

"Be sure, love; exhibitionism is like a drug, once you begin, well…"

Killian's words faded off as a blush of pink stained Alana's pale, white skin. She only hesitated a moment before she gave a short, sharp nod and whispered, "I'm sure."

The smile that spread across Killian's face was heart-stopping, for Doug, so he could only imagine how Alana's body responded. "I would be honored to *watch*."

"Thank you, Killian," she murmured, staring up at him as though he had just performed some sort of heavenly miracle. Doug winced at the adoration on her face. Perhaps getting her involved with Killian wasn't the best idea, but it was too late to back out now. His wife had asked him to fulfill her fantasy, and he'd be damned if he was going to let her down.

Responding only with a wide smile and a dip of his head, Killian moved to the loveseat nearby, and Doug's heart leapt in his chest. Finally! He would finally be allowed to live out his fantasy of public sex—and with his wife, no less! He couldn't resist skimming his hand up the curve of her hip to her shoulder. Her bare skin under the thin strap of her dress was as soft as cashmere, and he danced his fingers delicately up her neck and over to her zipper.

He felt her trembling under his hand as he lowered it one inch at a time, exposing her perfect pale, peach-colored skin. Flicking his eyes up to meet Killian's, he smiled when his partner twirled his finger in the air, directing the scene even from six feet away. Doug complied, by gently turning Alana around to face him, with her zipper halfway down her back, and her dress straps slipping off of her shoulders. The excitement on her face was tempered with apprehension in her touch as she placed her palms on Doug's chest awaiting his next move.

"I love you, sweetheart," he whispered just before capturing her lips under his own. Seeking only to soothe her nerves, he stroked his tongue over her soft skin, and then pushed his way into her sweet mouth.

~ ~ ~

Alana…

It was the ultimate rush. She could feel the zip of anxiety over her skin and the fire of desire in her blood. Alana had never felt more human. In the past, Doug had tried to get her to join in, but each time, something held her back.

Ultimately, she feared rejection. What if she wasn't passionate enough, or sexy enough, or thin enough for the crowd to want to watch? If she was honest with herself, her biggest fear was being rejected by the man who now watched her from a few feet away. She had no fear of rejection at the moment though, as he sat there taking her in with eyes that held green flames of need. Killian had always looked at her with appreciation, but never gave her any sign that he wanted her until tonight.

Tonight, he'd gone out of his way to lay his hand on her upper thigh during dinner. Doug had been occupied in conversation as his best friend made his desire known, but she didn't feel guilty about it. She'd seen the looks Doug gave his business partner when he thought no one was watching, and she'd heard him call out Killian's name in the darkness of their bedroom. So, she allowed herself to accept the pleasure Killian offered without a word.

His fingers had teased her skin through the thigh-high slit in her dress, and her thighs parted in an instinctive welcome. When his thick fingertip finally found her slit, she bit her own tongue to avoid begging him to finger fuck her then and there. He had only dallied for a moment before they were interrupted by the mass exodus at the end of the meal, but it was enough to light a bonfire in her belly. Even now, her thighs were damp with her own juices, and her clit was throbbing.

Doug drew her focus back to the present by nipping at her lower lip, and she felt her knees wobble underneath her. God, she loved it when he added a touch of pain. She could almost feel Killian's eyes on her, and she wondered briefly if anyone else in the room was watching. She felt Doug slide her zipper the rest of the way down, until it rested at the top of her ass crack. The cool air whispered over her skin, and she shivered as the garment free from her body. It pooled at her feet leaving her standing in just a strapless black bra and panties, and a black garter belt holding up silk stockings. She held her breath when he bit the tendon at the juncture of her neck and shoulder, realizing that she was now nearly nude in front of Killian. It was a delicious, wanton feeling. She let her head fall backwards, giving Doug the room he needed to suckle and nip at her throat.

His hand slid over the curve of her belly to the spread of her thighs, and he brushed his knuckles across the lacy crotch of her panties, drawing the first moan from her throat. Blood pounded in her ears, and her eyes drifted closed as his other hand pushed the foam cups of her bra down, exposing her breasts to view. Her nipples tightened into sharp points, and he latched onto one sending her senses reeling.

~ ~ ~

Killian…

Killian couldn't believe his luck. For months he had rocked a hard-on for Alana and Doug. From the first time they attended one of his Lusty Fantasies parties, he'd always known they were destined to be his, and he was a patient man. He waited, and watched, easing them along the path he wanted them to walk until they were right here, right now.

With Doug sucking his wife's tits a few feet in front of him, Killian tipped his glass, emptying the remaining half-inch of whiskey into his mouth and swallowing the burn. It was fortification for the control he was struggling to maintain. Right now, he wanted nothing more than to call the two of them to his side and force them both to their knees in front of him. After dipping his finger into Alana's juicy pussy at dinner, he knew she would be more than willing, but how would Doug react? Would he fly off the handle if Killian shoved his cock in his face and told him to suck it?

One way or another, tonight they were going to find out. He was tired of waiting, and watching Alana with her wide eyes, and Doug with his flushed cheeks, as they explored their exhibitionist sides. It was time to up the ante, and expose their submissive nature, too.

Doug had tossed Alana's bra completely aside so he could play with her tits. The long line of her spine and the sexy curve of her ass beckoned Killian, but he held his place and directed Doug to spin her around again.

His first view of her luscious breasts made his mouth water and his balls draw up tight. She had melon-sized tits with fat nipples that would look amazing pierced. They were a dusky rose color, with areolas the size of a half-dollar. Doug's hands cupped her and she arched her back, pushing her breasts out to Killian.

It took everything he had to resist the offering.

They were drawing the attention of some of the other guests, but Killian knew that no one would interrupt or distract the two putting on the show. If nothing else, this group was a safe haven for exploration. Everyone here had indulged in a fetish or fantasy at one time or another. A private invitation was necessary to gain access, and upon stepping through the front door, each guest was required to sign a waiver and confidentiality agreement before they were allowed to join the party.

He wanted to protect his friends, but he was also protecting himself. One day soon he would sit atop the *Fortune 500* list, and he'd be damned if a scandal would keep him from it.

Alana moaned and drew his attention back to the show. Doug was on his knees, pulling her panties over her hips, exposing her slit. Killian was pleased to see her bald pussy was dripping with need, and he rubbed at his own cock, mimicking Doug's touch on her body.

The man seemed to know his wife's body well as he suckled and nipped at various points on her inner thighs and down to the back of her knees. Wearing just the garter belt and hose now, Alana looked magnificent. Her plump lips were parted, and her firm tits lifted and fell with the increase in her breathing. She was a goddess among commoners, standing proudly before them displaying the passion filling her soul.

Satisfaction ripped through Killian when Doug looked over his shoulder at him, and then paused as though waiting for direction. Meeting Doug's dark gaze, Killian licked his lips just to see the other man's reaction. As expected, Doug's own tongue duplicated the action signaling his growing desire. His submissive nature was shining like an aura around him, and Killian jumped at the chance to take control.

"Taste her."

Chapter Two

Doug...

Doug's heart nearly stopped because of two words. Or maybe it wasn't the two words so much as the voice that said them. Killian's green eyes were flashing, and his jaw was tight. Was his hand cupping his cock?

Heart skipping, Doug dipped his tongue into the valley of Alana's labia. It came back covered in her pearly juice and he groaned. He could feel her thighs trembling under his palms as he pushed her legs wider. Damn, he loved the feeling of silk on her skin. The thigh-highs acted as a picture frame, displaying her delicious cunny perfectly to his intruding tongue.

Pushing his finger and thumb between the plump labia, he spread her open so that he could see her clit poking its head up. Cream pooled in her opening, and he wasted no time scooping it out with his tongue while his fingers pinched her clit.

Her moan of pleasure echoed through the now quiet room. When had everyone stopped talking? Doug resisted the urge to pull away from her and look to see who was watching them. The only person who truly mattered was Killian.

His dick twitched behind his zipper as the image of Killian's hand covering his groin filled his brain again. He wasn't about to consider why that turned him on so much. Doug knew how beautiful Alana was, with her soft-as-satin skin, and full-bodied curves. Her wide hips and deep cleavage never failed to rock his world, so why would it be any different for Killian?

Her fingers settled on the top of his head, digging into his scalp for balance, and he urged her on. That little bite of pain only served to fan his flames higher, and she knew it.

"Play with your tits, Alana," Killian instructed from behind Doug. He could have been next to him the words were so loud in Doug's brain. Her hands jerked away from his head as she followed the instructions, and he pulled back to see what Killian was seeing.

Alana's head was thrown back, her long blonde hair streaming down her back, eyes closed, lips parted. Her hands cupped her breasts but could never truly hold the massive globes. The stark black of her garter belt and hose made her skin seem luminescent and drew attention to her slit grinning back at him.

"Don't stop Doug, she wants your mouth on her," Killian said.

Without hesitation, Doug dropped his mouth back onto her spread pussy and resumed eating her out. He knew what she liked. Soft circles on her clit with the tip of his tongue, then a hard shove into her passage with a couple of fingers, and…

~ ~ ~

Alana…

Alana cried out as she orgasmed for the first time in front of an entire room full of people. Her pussy throbbing, and her skin tingling, she shuddered and struggled to keep from collapsing to the floor. Doug's hands gripped her waist firmly, and she eased into his chest as he rose to hold her. Keeping her eyes shut tightly, she rode out the remaining ripples of climax, all the while wondering what she'd been thinking.

After a few moments, people began to murmur as the conversations around them resumed, and her eyes opened to find only Killian still focused on the pair of them.

"That was beautiful, love."

His words eased her conscience, and she lifted her head to meet first his and then Doug's eyes, his mouth still wet with her desire and his full cheeks flushed bright pink. She could feel his rock hard erection pressed against her stomach, and a flame of lust burned in her belly.

"You are absolute perfection, Alana." Killian's hand brushed her hair away from her cheek, and she turned to face him. Dark and dangerous, that's what he was to her. Blonde-streaked brown hair, and dilated pupils, paired with a powerfully built body in that black and white tuxedo. As if he could hear her thoughts, his lips curled up in a smile. "But the night isn't over yet, is it Alana?"

A rush of anticipation filled her chest. He wanted her. As much as she loved her husband, she had been smitten with Killian since the moment she was introduced to him. How many times had she caught herself leaving one of his parties with the desire to ask him to join them burning on her lips?

Unable to speak, she shook her head and received a sexy smile from both men as a reward. Killian moved in close to her bare back, sandwiching her between their two bodies, and she shivered with anticipation.

She held her breath when Killian's arms came around her midsection, pinning Doug's against her sides. Doug's hand became caught between Killian's hips and her ass. She felt him squeezing her cheeks when his partner's hard cock came into contact with his knuckles, and she instinctively shifted her pelvis backwards to increase the friction.

God, she wanted that cock inside of her so bad...

"Now that we've proved you've got a wild streak, you need to tell us how far you're planning on taking this scene, sweetheart," Doug said. She could see the flexing muscle of his jawline, and she wondered what was going through his head. He had to know it was Killian's cock he was touching. If he could be that open-minded, then she could be as well.

Determined to ask for what she wanted, she swallowed hard, and said out loud, "I want you. Both of you."

The two men both reacted, squeezing her between their steely cocks and firm bodies. Killian pressed his nose into her hair, and she heard him inhale as he gently kissed the skin behind her ear. Doug kissed her forehead at the same time, completing the triad in an unusually intimate connection.

"Do you want to take this somewhere more private?" Doug murmured to her, and she quickly nodded.

Even though it turned her on to feel all of those eyes on her nude body, she was desperate to be fucked, and she wasn't quite ready to share that with the group yet. Killian held them in place when they would have moved to leave the room, and she turned to look at him over her shoulder.

~ ~ ~

Killian...

The Dominant in Killian fought with his inner voyeur for control of the situation. As much as he wanted to protect his new toys, he also wanted to show them off. He was a dirty, perverted man, with wicked fantasies that he chose to embrace, and he loved watching sin almost as much as he loved committing it. All around him, friends and business acquaintances milled around seeking to fulfill their fantasies for the night, or just getting off on the one happening in front of them. It was important to give the partygoers a show, without revealing too much of oneself because, come Monday morning, they would all put on their ties, and button up their pressed shirts as they returned to the corporate world.

Everything changed for Killian when Alana asked for what she wanted. The moment he heard her say the words, he realized she meant them. It inflated his ego and dampened his enthusiasm for exhibitionism at the same time, but he wasn't quite ready to let her run away from her darkest desires like a scared little bunny. In fact, he wanted to see how far he could push her.

Tipping her head back with a tug on her long blonde locks, he met Doug's eyes in question. This was her husband's last opportunity to dictate the situation, and the moment he nodded the go-ahead, Killian captured Alana's moist lips with his own, finally tasting the sin on her tongue he'd dreamed about for months. She was a wicked combination of honey, scotch, and woman. If he was a weaker man he might have taken her right then and there without the necessary dance of foreplay.

Forcing his mouth away from hers with a sharp nip to her bottom lip, he stared down into her clear blue eyes. Shifting his body, Killian purposely grazed Doug's hands and her ass with his cloth covered-cock as he spoke to her.

"Just a minute, love. I think Doug deserves a reward for indulging you tonight. What do you say?"

His words filled the air around them with heavy tension, as she debated how to respond. He could see her reservations, as well as the bonfire of desire they lit as she bit that succulent bottom lip and turned back to Doug.

To Doug's credit, he managed to keep his mouth shut and let her think through all of the possibilities without swaying her one way or the other, again reassuring Killian that he'd been right about their dual submissive desires.

Training them was going to be a delight if they continued to be so responsive to each other and to him. He could already see matching collars adorning their throats at the next Lusty Fantasies party. Just the thought of placing his collar on either one of them made his heart and his cock twitch. How would they feel about a permanent threesome?

To his surprise, Alana nodded to herself and gave him a bright smile before she began sliding down his body.

~ ~ ~

Alana…

Alana could feel Killian's hot breath on the side of her face, and his huge hands blanketed her softly rounded tummy. For once in her life, she didn't worry about the rolls or stretch marks there. All she could see was the desire that lit up her husband's eyes. Doug still wanted her, and now Killian wanted her, too. When was the last time she truly felt desirable? It had been years.

For fifteen years she had slept with the same man, in the same bed, in the same home, never asking for more. But tonight, there was something special in the air, and she felt completely reckless. It tempted her into asking Doug for this foray into exhibitionism, and now it taunted her with the sexy man pressed against her back.

Killian was everything that Doug wasn't— confident, rugged, and dangerous. She loved Doug with all her heart, but he was more submissive than she at times and, although he wasn't out of shape, he certainly wasn't as taut and lean as his business partner. She wondered silently how far apart they were in age as she felt Killian's lips brush the back of her neck and Doug's fingers kneading her fleshy ass. It wasn't an important fact, so she let the curiosity fizzle in light of the burning embers of desire that were sizzling in her stomach. She needed this.

Slowly, and without pushing them apart, she slid down their bodies to her knees. Doug was average height at five foot ten, and Killian only topped him by two inches, so she was very comfortable resting on her haunches between the two of them. In fact, they were at the perfect height. Twisting, she angled her body until she was sideways between them, and with one reassuring glance up at Killian, she reached for Doug's zipper first.

~ ~ ~

Doug...

Alana's fingers trailed over the ridge of his cock, making him burn for more, and he watched in stunned fascination as she released his dick to view. He might not be as powerful or have as many connections as Killian in the business world, but Doug knew he had an advantage in the cock department on almost every man in the room. At nine inches fully erect, and almost three inches across in thickness, he had never disappointed a lady. Scared one away, yes, but disappointed? Never. Hell, if they measured it at that very moment, he guessed it was a half-inch longer than normal, because it was stretching to reach her perfectly pursed lips like it had a mind of its own.

Fisting his hands at his sides, he looked up to find Killian watching him instead of his wife, and a wave of nerves washed through him. They were supposed to be doing this for Alana, but the look on Killian's face certainly wasn't for her. When he dropped his head down, he saw Killian do the same out of his peripheral vision, and he caught the look of surprise as his friend took in his erect shaft.

Ego thoroughly inflated, Doug felt his chest fill with pride before he realized that Killian was fully focused on Alana again. Surely the look hadn't been anything more than a voyeuristic interest in Doug's reaction to his wife's new-found free thinking, a momentary lapse, he guessed. The nearly tangible lust in the air was getting to him.

At that moment, Alana gripped his thick cock, and delicately licked the sensitive tip. Hissing out a breath, he forced himself to stay upright, as she began to give him the best head of his life in a crowded room. He felt every pair of eyes turned on him, and watched his nearly nude wife on her knees as she serviced him. The eroticism was intoxicating, and he fought to hold onto the tendrils of his control. Fuck, he didn't want to embarrass himself by shooting off before he really enjoyed this moment.

Grasping her long hair in his fist, he jerked her head off of his cock with a loud pop. Her lips remained parted in an O of surprise, and her heavy-lidded eyes flipped up to meet his in question. "Don't thank me too much, sweetheart. I want this to last."

She smirked up at him, as though confident she could break his control without a second thought, and he felt a shiver of lust skip down his spine. It had always been this way between them. A shared dialogue of submission, first one and then the other would take control, but never a true Dominant/submissive partnership. Just mutual desires being fulfilled with an emotional connection.

Killian's hand suddenly laced itself over and around Doug's in Alana's hair, surprising them both, as he gently exerted pressure so that her mouth went back down to Doug's cock. "Don't stop her; it was just getting good, D. I want to know if she swallows or not."

Doug's eyes met Killian's over Alana's bobbing head, and Doug felt like he'd been gripped by the nutsack. If it wasn't for the steady pressure of Alana's hands braced on each thigh, he might have glanced down to check. There was an intense look of hunger in Killian's eyes again, and there was no denying who it was directed at when he made eye contact with him.

The realization that his best friend and business partner really was sexually attracted to him, broke his control, and without warning, Doug shot a full load of cum down Alana's throat. He heard her squeak of surprise as she nearly choked on the mouthful, but he could feel her relax, so that she could take it like a champ, while he maintained eye contact with the first man he'd ever wanted to fuck.

Chapter Three

Killian...

Without thinking, Killian reached out and drew his thumb across Alana's pursed lips, stealing a dribble of cum from the crease. He took his time as he licked it from the digit, maintaining eye contact with Doug the whole time. Heat flared in the other man's dark eyes, and his jaw flexed with tension. Satisfied that Doug was interested, Killian released him from his visual hold and turned back to Alana, who was still kneeling at their feet.

"That was beautiful, love. You've made your husband proud." When Doug didn't immediately agree, Killian frowned at him pointedly.

"Yes, of course sweetheart. I, uh, well...my brain just isn't functioning yet. I think you fried it with that blow job," Doug said with a sharp chuckle. His pants were still open and his dick hung limply just to the left of his zipper, the shimmer of saliva and semen catching the light and making Killian's cock throb.

"While I'm down here…" Alana said quietly. Her eyes zeroed in on Killian's zipper, but her hands stayed splayed on her thighs. She was completely relaxed as she sat in the submissive pose without realizing it.

Killian heard Doug's sharp inhale, but he didn't acknowledge it. Instead he stroked his hand over her golden hair, and drew her head closer to his hips. When her nose made contact with the hard length of his erection she shivered against him, and he felt a smile stretch his lips.

"Is there something you'd like to ask me, love?" His voice deepened, and her eyelids grew heavier at the gravelly sound.

"Um, can I, well… that is…do you want me to…"

"Say it, Alana." Doug demanded gruffly. Killian saw him stroke his cock as he watched Alana.

She flushed bright red, and dropped her head away from him. Killian hurried to reassure her, "Easy, love. Doug just wants you to accept yourself and ask for what you want. That is what you're here for right? And you're already brave enough to come this far. Ask me."

Her swollen lips parted as she took a deep breath, and mumbled, "Killian, may I suck your…cock? Please?"

The last word was the only reason Killian didn't make her repeat herself. She said it as a final plea to end her discomfort, both mental and physical. Need burned in her eyes when the blue orbs finally lifted to meet his. "You ask so prettily, love. Of course you may."

With shaking hands, she managed to release the zipper and button on his tuxedo pants, and his hard cock popped free. It wasn't nearly as thick as Doug's, but he only had him by an inch in length. Killian knew he was more than adequately endowed, and he stood proudly with his erection jutting from the nest of dark-haired curls between his thighs. Both Alana and Doug were fixated on the purple length, and under their twin gazes, it thickened even further.

"Don't make me wait, Alana. I'm not much for teasing." There was just enough of a threat in his voice to have her moving quickly to grasp his cock in her small, pale hand and stroke him firmly. Her technique needed refining, but she certainly made up for it with enthusiasm as she engulfed the head of his dick and sucked him to the back of her throat.

Taking a chance, Killian braced himself with a hand on Doug's bicep and used the other to grip the back of Alana's head. He was ridiculously pleased when neither resisted the intimate touch. Doug planted his feet, and used his opposite hand to cup his cock and balls, while he watched his wife suck Killian off. She relaxed further, allowing his prick to slide farther down her throat. She gagged a little, tears welling up in her eyes, and spittle leaking from the corner of her mouth. Killian eased his hold, and wiped the escaping tears from her cheeks with his thumb.

"Easy, love. I've got all night for you...two." He let the last word linger on his lips without looking up at Doug. He wanted to make sure he allowed the man plenty of room to stop the inevitable if it freaked him out.

Alana's tongue undulated against the underside of his shaft, and he felt a familiar tingle at the base of his balls. Sliding his hand under her chin, he gripped her jaw firmly and pulled her off of him. "Doug, move over here, and let's give her a challenge."

~ ~ ~

Doug…

Killian directed him and Alana where he wanted them, like an erotic puppeteer, pulling their strings as they danced for him. Before he really understood what was happening, Doug was hip-to-hip with him, and their cocks were slapping against each other. Precum dribbled from the twin mushroom heads, and Alana looked like a cobra entranced by a lone flute. She opened her mouth, but her lips only stretched so wide. There was no way that both dicks were going to fit in her small mouth.

Instead, she took turns, sliding her lips over first one, then the other. She pumped her fist up one length before she sucked her way down the next, with both cocks smashed together in her hands. It was a feast of kinky proportions and Doug was all in. He had never imagined having another man's junk so close to his, but he couldn't take his eyes off Killian's cock. It was perfectly shaped, and it curved upward slightly in offering.

Mentally slapping himself, he swallowed back a lump of shame. Surely it wasn't right for him to stand here fantasizing about tasting another man's cock while his wife had her lips around his own erection?

She vacuum-sealed her lips tight around the crown of his cock and he shuddered, reaching a hand out to steady himself without realizing he had placed it on the small of Killian's back. When it hit him, it was too late to remove it without looking odd, so he left it there. There was something comforting about the heat that filtered through Killian's tux jacket.

Any other night, it would have taken Doug an hour to recharge his battery enough to come again, but the sexy tableau and the taboo of fucking in front of people he knew, had his cock vibrating with pent up desire again.

"Fuck, I'm going to come again, sweetheart."

"Do it," she whispered seductively. Her eyes met his then moved to meet Killian's, as she gripped both of their dicks in her hands and stroked them firmly. "Please, come for me."

The demand was sweetly erotic, but Doug waited. It wasn't until Killian firmly nodded his head that he realized he had been waiting for permission to come all over his own wife.

~ ~ ~

Alana...

She felt each twitch of the cocks in her palms. Killian's spurted harder, but Doug's went on for what seemed like an eternity, covering her cleavage in spunk and leaving her sticky and wet with her own desire.

It wasn't that she had forgotten they had an audience, but she had managed to block them out and focus her mind entirely on the two men in front of her. So when someone suddenly began to clap, it was a loud sharp sound that ricocheted through her brain. Embarrassment flooded her, and her eyes popped open as she shot to her feet, swaying on numb limbs that had been bent too long.

Doug's arms wrapped around her, with her sticky wet breasts pressed tightly to his dress shirt, the pale green tie she had carefully selected for him ruined now. She related to the limp material as she felt the shame of her actions building like a thunderstorm in her head, pounding at her conscience and seizing up her heart.

Like a lighthouse on the horizon, Killian's face appeared in front of her wild, darting gaze, blocking out the room and the audience completely. Instead of hearing their applause and murmured chatter, she heard Doug shushing her and Killian firmly saying her name.

"Alana. Look at me." Her eyes found his, and she held on to his steady gaze as tightly as her arms held onto her husband. "That's it. Good girl. Stay with us. None of them matter. The only people who matter are Doug and I, right love?"

She managed to nod, her teeth beginning to chatter as shock set in and she remembered she was standing in the middle of the crowded living room of Killian's home wearing only a garter belt, stockings and heels. Biting her lips, she fought to hold in the tears that were slipping from her eyes, but she was unable to hold onto her focus now that reality had set in.

Killian was frowning and she heard someone curse before she was lifted up into Doug's arms. The breeze of their movement was chilly on her flushed skin, but she was already shivering, so it went unnoticed. She hung limply in Doug's arms, her hands locked tight around his neck, and her face buried in his chest.

"Bring her in here. She needs some time to adjust and calm down."

"Is she okay? I've never seen her like this." Doug took a seat on something that sunk down—a bed she was guessing—and she heard a door click closed, cutting off the chattering of the party guests until the noise was nothing but a faint murmur through the walls.

"She'll be fine. She's just not used to being the center of attention, and she got lost in the moment. Reality's a bitch when you're that turned on."

"Tell me about it."

Alana could hear the two of them discussing her as though she wasn't there, but she couldn't make her mouth work to speak up. Humiliation and disappointment burned in her gut. This was supposed to be her moment to be free of her hang-ups, the moment she let go of her self-doubts and embraced her sensuality. Instead, she felt like a wannabe porn star that got carried away when the director yelled 'cut'.

"I should've said no." Doug sounded so forlorn and broken that she forced her eyes open to stare up at his jaw.

Killian inhaled sharply, "No, you should not have. She asked for what she wanted because she is stronger than you realize. She's just having a momentary panic attack, but she'll be back to herself again in a few moments. It's something that happens a lot when a new sub does a public scene for the first time. Some realize they can handle it, while others make it a hard limit."

"I'm not a sub," she whispered, turning her head to glare at Killian.

His sexy full lips turned up in a half grin, and he nodded, "Of course not, love. My mistake. You're only submissive for me."

Her eyes widened and she felt Doug staring down at her, waiting for her to respond. "I-I'm not sure what I am, but I know I'm not an exhibitionist. When I realized all of those people were around me, and they had just watched me sucking...well, let's just say I think I'm content to cross public sex off my bucket list."

She was feeling more like herself and her body relaxed and warmed as she lay in Doug's arms. It didn't bother her like it probably should have to be naked in front of Killian. Instead, she felt as comfortable with him as she did with her husband. As she mulled that over, Killian moved closer to where the pair sat on the bed, moving in tight, so that the soft fabric of his trousers brushed against her naked hip and Doug's knees.

"Can you honestly tell me that you weren't turned on, Alana?" he asked with a raised eyebrow of doubt.

She shook her head, "No. I was most definitely turned on, but not because they were watching me." The room was heavy with tension as both men waited for her to continue. Alana struggled for a brief moment before she forced the words out. "I was turned on because *you* were watching me."

"Me?" Killian asked.

Nodding, she waited for the fallout from that bomb, but it never came. Doug pressed a kiss to her temple and nuzzled her ear, while Killian stood there watching the two of them mutely as he processed her words.

"You want me to watch you."

"No." she said shortly, frowning, "I want you with me. With me and Doug." Her eyes lifted to meet Doug's. "I know this is a shock to you, too, because I've never let on that things weren't perfect between us, but I didn't realize how much was missing until now. I'm so sorry for my freak out, but I really think I need this. Can you give me tonight? If you ask me to walk away in the morning and never speak of it again, I will, but please, can we start over, and finish this night with Killian?"

Chapter Four

Doug...

It took him a moment to register what she was asking. Alana wanted to keep going. She wanted to fuck Killian. Holy shit! It was like heaven and hell were both tempting him with what he wanted the most.

He lifted his eyes to meet Killian's. They were business partners, but Doug considered him to be his best friend, too. How would tonight change that? Did it matter?

The heat of two sets of eyes bore into him as he tried to formulate a response that didn't sound too eager, but didn't stop them either.

"Do you want this?" he asked Killian.

Killian's response started with a slow sexy smile that lit up his face, and darkened his green eyes. Without a word, he slid the tuxedo jacket from his shoulders, and tossed it onto a chair across the room. Then his long fingers began working at the knot of his bow tie. He was so close to them that Doug could feel his movements against his knees, and it kept his blood just slightly below the boiling point.

It was time to face the elephant in the room. "This is for Alana, and we can't promise you more than tonight."

Killian paused with the black satin bow tie dangling from his fingers. They all three stared at it motionless and silent. It was wrinkled from wear, and yet parts of it were perfectly pristine. What a perfect metaphor for their current predicament.

"I don't want your promises." Killian spoke barely above a whisper, but his voice echoed through the room. "I want your submission."

Doug's eyes shot to Alana, and he was surprised to find her heavy-lidded and flushed. Oh yeah, she was certainly into that plan. With a smile, he turned back to Killian. "It looks like she's okay with that."

"I know she is, but are you?"

~ ~ ~

Alana...

"Me?" Doug squeaked, and then cleared his throat. "What do you mean?"

Alana almost felt sorry for her husband. He was clearly clueless about his own best friend. She'd had her suspicions that Killian was a Dom, but he confirmed it when he took control of the scene in the other room. It turned her on like crazy; she desperately wanted to submit to him, but she had a gut feeling he wouldn't go for it unless Doug was on his knees too.

"I mean, I'm in charge. What I say goes when we're in here. If you don't like it you can say stop and we all part as friends, no harm no foul. But if you stay, you give up control to me."

He said it so calmly that they might have been discussing the Sunday newspaper, but Alana could see the flames he held tightly under control deep in his emerald eyes, Killian wanted both of them. He wanted to Master them, and possibly even fuck them both. A shiver of desire skittered up her spine, and her pussy dripped onto Doug's slacks. She wanted that. Desperately.

"Please say yes, Doug. Try it." She murmured, kissing his jaw, and wriggling her ass on his groin.

He let out a low groan, and his brow wrinkled as if he was in pain. "I'm not sure."

"Of course you're not. Most submissives aren't sure until they've experienced submission for the first time. Trust me to guide you in this. I've been doing it most of my life." Killian's demeanor was alluring, almost mesmerizing. His hand came up, and he stroked Alana's cheek softly, "We can please her together, but the only way I'll get enjoyment out of it, is if I have complete control."

"I'm not a submissive."

Alana couldn't hold in her laughter, and she only laughed harder when Doug glared at her like Grumpy Cat. "I'm sorry, honey. You know I love you madly, but you are most definitely submissive in the bedroom."

Doug looked so put out that she felt guilty for teasing him. "I'm not sure this is a good idea," he grumbled, moving her off his lap and onto the bed beside them.

He stood, but Killian didn't back away. Instead the two were chest-to-chest, face-to-face, groin-to-groin facing off. "What are you scared of?"

Killian's question seemed to take Doug by surprise and he fumbled for an answer. Alana rose up on her knees behind him, pressing her breasts against his broad back. Doug relaxed slightly between the two of them, and she took it as an invitation, reaching around to slide her hand into the opening of his slacks to grip his semi-hard cock.

"I don't know what you want from me," Doug said, almost whimpering, as she pushed her hand deeper to cup his balls, and Killian's hand replaced hers on his cock. Doug jumped at the first touch of the other man's hand, but then groaned loudly.

"What do I want from you?" Killian repeated, meeting Alana's eyes over Doug's shoulder in triumph as Doug's head fell backward in acquiescence. "Everything."

Chapter Five

Killian...

His chest felt heavy where it met Doug's, and the firm length of Doug's cock in his hand made Killian's heart skip a beat. He had exactly what he wanted in the palm of his hand. Doug was relaxing under his touch, and Alana was wild with desire as her fingers tangled with his around her husband's erection.

"Say yes, Doug." Killian prompted. There was no way he was going to move forward without a direct answer. He wouldn't risk Doug trying to say he was coerced into this.

"Yes."

The word had a ripple effect on all three of them. Alana moaned, and bit Doug's shoulder. Doug gasped, and braced his hands on Killian's chest to stay standing, and Killian had to grind his teeth together to keep from forcing Doug to his knees immediately; that wouldn't win him any points at the moment.

"As of now you're both mine until morning, your safe word is *dawn*, because that's the soonest I'll let you go without it. Are we clear?" Killian slipped into his Dom voice easily, and Alana and Doug responded to it. She piped up with a "Yes Sir," while Doug nodded his head vigorously. "Sir, Doug. You'll call me Sir when we're in the bedroom."

"Yes...Sir." He whispered it, but it was enough. Killian's blood pressure skyrocketed and he gave Doug's dick a hard squeeze before reaching for Alana. It was important to ease Doug into this, but he knew Alana was ready for it.

She moved easily for him, coming to rest on her knees in front of him, thighs spread, head bowed, hands behind her back. It was a beautiful sight. She had glorious curves and pale skin that glowed softly with a pink flush of desire. Moving away from her, Killian flipped on a floor lamp across the room so that he could see them both better. Now he could see the pink stain on Doug's cheeks, and the glistening tip of his big cock jutting up in welcome.

"Have you been trained as a submissive, Alana?"

"No Sir, but I've read enough erotic novels to know what to expect," she responded, keeping her head down.

Killian frowned at her, "I doubt you could learn anything about real BDSM in a novel, but perhaps I'll have to borrow a few books from your library."

She lifted her head, and he could see her teasing smile. "Of course. I have plenty for you to choose from, Sir."

"And you, Doug? What do you know about being a submissive?"

The way Doug stood with his head resting lazily on his shoulders, and his hips jutting forward, he almost looked drugged. It was possible he was already on the verge of subspace. That certainly wouldn't do. They had at least four hours until dawn, and Killian was determined to make use of every minute.

"I only know what I've seen in porn, and what Alana has told me."

That surprised him. "You two have discussed this?"

"Not exactly," Alana said, throwing an irritated look at Doug, "He likes it when I read him parts of my books while we're in bed." When Killian frowned at her, she hurried to add a "Sir" onto the end of her explanation.

"You do have a sexy voice, love. I can see why he would want to listen to you say the nastiest words possible."

Killian and Doug shared a smile when Alana blushed again and mumbled, "Thank you, Sir."

"You're welcome. I think we'll skip the scene and get to the fucking. My cock is hard enough to pound nails. Alana, help Doug get his clothes off, and remove your stockings and garter belt before they get torn apart." Killian watched as the couple worked in tandem to remove every wisp of fabric from between them. When the pair was completely naked, they turned back to him, Alana with a sweet sensual smile, Doug with a challenging tilt to his chin. "Beautiful. You're an attractive couple, but you already know that. Doug, help Alana onto the bed, and use this to blindfold her." He passed Doug a scarf retrieved from the bureau nearby.

Alana's pleasure at his directive was obvious as she nearly leapt onto the king size bed and lifted her head so that Doug could loop the silk fabric around her head.

"Perfect." Killian tugged at his own dress shirt, popping a few buttons as he hastily removed the garment, and then tossed it carelessly onto the chair holding his jacket. "Have you ever fucked her tits, Doug?"

"Many times. She's got fantastic tits."

"Mm-hmm, she certainly does." Killian toed off his shoes, and dropped his trousers, leaving them piled on the floor as he moved closer to his bed. He kept his gaze steady on Doug even as the other man surveyed his body. "Don't forget your manners, pet, or I'll have to discipline you. Remember, you agreed to be mine for the night."

Doug flinched, but nodded, "Yes, Sir."

~ ~ ~

Doug…

Killian's words were a reminder of his place in this event, and Doug felt it to his core. This wasn't going to be some sort of fling they would all walk away from in the morning completely unscathed. Something in Killian's tone told him that he would be completely changed by dawn. The question was, would they ever be able to go back after this?

Retrieving something from the night table, Killian joined them on the bed. His cock was standing proudly, and Doug felt a rush of heat to his loins as his mouth watered. What would he taste like?

"Get her nipples good and hard, pet. She's looking lonely."

Killian's instruction seemed to ground Doug back into reality, and he focused on teasing his wife's breasts and nipples until she was rocking her hips and whimpering underneath him.

"Good, that's enough."

Resting back on his heels, Doug watched as Killian slipped small black nipple clamps onto each of Alana's fat nipples. She yelped when the first one snapped in place, but she only gasped when the second one was fitted. They looked sexy as hell. Her areolas were a dusky rose color, while her nipples, trapped by the clamps, quickly became a darker maroon. Reaching out to stroke one of them, Doug caught himself just in time, and lifted his eyes to Killian for permission. He wasn't ready to consider what the look of triumph on his best friend's face might mean. Instead, he took advantage of the opportunity and caressed the tips of his wife's aching breasts.

"That's intense!" Alana gasped, shivering as goose bumps popped up all over her body. Killian just chuckled next to her.

"Oh, love, we haven't even begun. What was it you asked me earlier? To *watch* you? Do you still want me to just watch, Alana?" Killian teased. While Doug occupied himself with her nipples, Killian was running his hand over her soft belly and thick thighs, spreading her legs wider so that he could skim a finger along her juicy pussy lips.

She was breathing hard when she answered, "No, Sir. Please don't just watch."

Doug couldn't remember ever seeing his wife so wantonly sexual before. Sure, she was a passionate woman and they had a good sex life, but this was something altogether different. It was like she had been encapsulated in a cocoon for the last fifteen years and was suddenly breaking out to spread her wings.

Killian was moving between her legs, spreading her open with his big hands. It was distracting to watch, and Doug had to fight to maintain his concentration and play with her nipples.

"Alana, you're going to lie still while Doug fucks those glorious breasts of yours, and I feast on your cunt. Don't move, love." That was all the instruction he gave before he lowered his mouth to her waiting pussy. Doug watched, fascinated as she tensed but remained in place. He'd never seen her hold still during sex. There were times when he was licking her cunt that he had to hold onto both of her hips like handlebars because she bucked so hard, but with just one demand from Killian, she had completely changed her ways.

Killian's eyes met his, and Doug instinctively knew he was disappointed in the delay. He was supposed to be fucking Alana's tits. Not much of a hardship, but if he straddled her body to do it right his bare ass and balls would be almost right in Killian's face. Surely that's not what he intended?

Pulling his face away from his task, Killian slapped Alana's thigh lightly when she let out a whimper of protest. "What's the problem?"

"I'm just…I've never…well…if I get on top of her, you'll be staring at my ass." Doug finally said in a rush. He heard Alana fighting to hold back a titter of laughter, but he refused to look up to see how Killian was reacting.

"That's exactly what's supposed to happen, pet. You have no need to feel self-conscious. You have a nice ass for a man your age," Killian said. The look on his face was steady when Doug's eyes shot up to meet his.

"A man my age?"

"Good, now I have your attention. When I said I wanted your submission, Doug, I meant in everything. Not just when you feel comfortable, so either safeword out and Alana will rejoin you at home in the morning, or get your ass up there and fuck your wife's tits."

Doug moved quickly. He never even considered safewording so that he could leave. He climbed up on top of Alana, and pressed her soft breasts tight around his hard length. Something cold brushed against his shoulder, and he turned to find Killian passing him a bottle of lube. Within moments he was lubed up and fucking away, without a thought for the man behind him who was lapping up his wife's cream while he was getting an eyeful of Doug's ass.

~ ~ ~

Alana…

She was fighting her own body to stay still. Killian's hands were warm on her inner thighs, and his tongue was searing hot on her clit. He circled the sensitive button gently and then moved his tongue in a rapid-fire movement over it, before switching it up again to lick her in long deep strokes from top to bottom. It was a masterful dance he did, and she was dying to come all over him.

Meanwhile, her husband rode her breasts, his fat cock slurping in the deep valley of her cleavage as though his life depended on it. She knew this was one of his favorite alternatives when she wasn't feeling up to actual fucking, but with her nipples clamped and Killian's mouth on her pussy, she was turned on as hell by his steady thrusting.

Her fingers dug into the bedspread until she felt her fingernails bend. Thrashing her head, she whimpered, "Please!" She began to tremble underneath them.

A hand covered hers where it was clamped down on the bedspread, and she relaxed her grip, allowing Killian to draw her palm up to Doug's ass. She knew it was Killian because Doug would never ask her to grab his ass, and by the pressure on her fingertips, she knew he wanted her to spread her husband's cheeks open.

Shit, the man was multi-talented. He was still teasing her pussy with his mouth, while he instructed her with his hands. She followed his lead, skimming her fingers down the split of Doug's ass, even when he slowed his thrusting. Expecting him to resist, she eased back to massage his cheeks until he was back to full throttle on her tits. Once he had resumed his motions, she resumed hers. She pressed her fingertips between his spread ass cheeks, exploring a valley she had never been allowed to before, by touch alone.

He tensed when she pushed against his forbidden hole, but when he didn't stop her she continued to rub gentle circles over that sensitive opening until it relaxed enough for her to insert just the tip of her finger. That was when she lost her concentration.

There was no way she could keep her hips still any longer with the glorious action happening on her clit, her finger in Doug's ass, and his cock mashed between her breasts. With a scream, she launched upwards, her movement lifting them all a couple of inches as she shattered underneath them.

Chapter Six

Killian...

Killian took control, without missing a beat after easing Alana down from her climax. Seeing her finger in Doug's tiny back hole had him dribbling pre-cum all over the bedspread, and he knew it was time to take action.

Doug was still pumping away between her breasts, but after two orgasms earlier in the evening, he was likely to stay that way for a while. Killian rose up to his knees, cupping Doug's ass to shift him forward, so that his aching cock could slide against Alana's dripping snatch.

"Mmm, your wife has a hot pussy, Doug." Killian groaned sinking his cock halfway into her tight sheath before he had to stop and give her time to adjust.

"Fuck yeah, she does. Don't go easy on her. She likes it rough...uh...Sir." Doug was looking back over his shoulder, watching Killian slide his dick into Alana instead of thrusting his own cock between her breasts.

Killian was glad to see his comfort level was still high considering his back passageway had already been invaded. Pushing limits was Killian's specialty, and these two made him ache to cross every line they drew in the sand.

Gripping Alana's hip with one hand, Killian grabbed ahold of Doug's shoulder with the other, and began to thrust. He knew that it would give Doug the sensation of being fucked every time he pushed forward, and he delighted in watching the other man squirm atop his wife.

Doug grunted, and his body tensed, but he didn't push Killian's hand away. Surprisingly, he released his grip on Alana's breasts, and covered Killian's hand with his own. A shot of heat zipped through the connection, and Killian immediately made a few decisions about how far he was going to push Doug.

"Does she squirt?" Killian asked, his voice harsher than he intended.

"Nope, but that doesn't stop you from trying." Doug said, and they shared a wicked grin.

Killian rocked his hips, forcing his cock up against Alana's g-spot, and bracing her ass on his knees. With the hand that had been holding her hip, he used his thumb to find her clit, and he pressed gently. Her body shuddered under him, and he did it again more firmly. By the time she climaxed again he was barely holding onto his control, and there wasn't a chance in hell he would be able to bring her to the top again without coming all over her.

"No luck this time, love," he told her, pressing a kiss to her belly, close enough to Doug's ass cheeks to feel his hair displace against them, "But I don't give up easily. Up with you now."

~ ~ ~

Alana...

Once they had all separated their tangle of limbs, Killian lifted the blindfold away. She had to blink at the sudden flood of light in her eyes, but once she was able to focus again, her vision was filled with nothing but delicious man meat.

Killian was as well-built as she anticipated, with abs that had more ridges than a potato chip, and a sexy line of brown hair that ran in a narrow strip from his nipples to his nads. Beside him Doug was stockier, and less defined, but no less attractive. His bare chest was adorned with a single tattoo that said, *Only the Good Die Young*, homage to his younger years and the best friend he lost when he was seventeen. It had always been their sexy secret. Very few people knew he had the black filigreed lettering over his left peck, but now Killian was one of them. How long would Doug allow him to remain in their circle after tonight?

"There you are gorgeous. As much fun as blindfolding is, I love seeing your eyes," Doug said, kissing her deeply. She loved tasting herself on his lips from earlier. If he wasn't coated in sticky lube, she might have kissed his cock for the pleasure it brought her breasts.

Killian moved his face in close enough for both of them to feel his breath, and he took over the moment their lips separated. Through barely open eyes, Alana watched as Doug's lips brushed across his best friend's cheek as he pulled away. It was as close to a kiss as she figured he was going to give, and damn, it turned her on.

Alana rested on her elbows, while Killian removed the clamps from her nipples. It seemed to turn him on even more when she yelped in pain. Quickly, Doug sucked a nipple between his lips, while Killian laved the other with his tongue, easing the sting until her whimpers went from pain to pleasure.

After three orgasms, her limbs were limp as noodles, and she was struggling to keep herself from dozing as they licked and sucked her swollen aching nipples. Both men still had massive hard-ons, but she wasn't sure how she was possibly going to survive two more rounds of fucking.

Killian seemed to sense that she was giving out, and by the sticky line of precum dangling from the purple head of his cock, he was on the brink too. This time he directed Doug to lie on his back, and Alana to climb astride him. She didn't hesitate, climbing up into her favorite position, and reaching for his thick cock.

From her place atop him, she leaned over her husband, and pressed a sweet kiss to his parted lips. "Thank you for tonight," she whispered, "This has already been more than I ever could have dreamed."

"I love you, sweetheart. I would do anything to make you happy," he responded with a small smile. "Now get on, or that bossy Dom you like so much will be spanking us both."

She giggled when Killian growled back, "Don't tempt me."

~ ~ ~

Doug...

Doug relaxed on his back under Alana, enjoying the sexy way she looked at him through glassy eyes. He wasn't lying. He really would do anything to make her happy. Hell, he'd let her stick her finger up his ass for god's sake. Although, to be honest, that had felt pretty damn good once he got past the initial invasion.

"If you two keep talking, I'll make you suck me off, and leave you both hanging for the night." Killian's voice was sharp and demanding. Gone was the playful carefree man they had invited into the evening. His control was broken and, shockingly, that set butterflies fluttering in Doug's belly.

He wasn't expecting Killian to grip his cock before his wife could, and he had to focus everything he had, to keep from coming all over the place. The palm was slightly callused, and the grip was firmer than Alana's. All in all, he fucking loved it.

The firm way Killian held him gave him the impression that he wasn't just lining things up down there. He was proved right when Alana's breasts were suddenly blanketing his face, and the silk cloth that had been used to blindfold his wife, stroked over the length of his dick wiping away the lube that coated it. His confusion was cleared when Killian's mouth wrapped around his cock a moment later. He heard himself let out a deep moan and his hips lurched upward, forcing the head of his dick deeper into Killian's throat. The man took it like a pro, relaxing his throat so that it could slide in easily. Then he wriggled his tongue against the thick ridge that ran on the underside, making Doug whimper.

Even the huge tits draping his face and puffy nipples dragging over his lips couldn't distract him from the blowjob. It was like nothing he'd ever had before. Alana was always careful to keep her teeth away from him; Killian was anything but careful. He seemed to make a point of scraping his teeth down the length of him with every thrust. It was mind-blowing, and Doug inhaled sharply feeling the release building in his balls. Just when he would have let go and poured himself down Killian's throat, a hand wrapped around the base of his shaft and squeezed tightly, cutting off the rush.

"Fuck!" he cursed loudly, pushing upwards with his hips as though he could dislodge the hand.

"Not yet. Come, love, climb on." Killian released Doug's cock, and Alana was tugged back into position. With a hard thrust of his hips, Doug found her sweet spot and sunk blissfully deep into her soft, slick heat.

It wasn't long before the two of them were humping wildly against each other, reaching for their orgasms. Doug stared up at his wife as she bounced on top of him, her head thrown back so that her shoulder rested on Killian's chest, but the moment that Killian met his eyes Doug knew he was up to something. A wicked look of sin filled his green eyes, and made Doug fumble his steady fucking motion. Just long enough for Killian to tip Alana forward, and push both of Doug's thighs up and back.

"Hey! What the hell?" Doug fought to maintain his line of sight to Killian, but Alana's hair fell in his face, blocking his view.

"Easy, Doug. I won't do anything you don't want me to," Killian said, just before his cockhead pressed against Doug's exposed asshole.

"Wait! What are you..."

Killian cut him off by rubbing the head of his erection hard against Doug's tight pucker. The combination of lube from Alana's fingers a few minutes ago, and Killian's lube-covered cock, proved to be too much for Doug's anal muscles. They spread open with a burning pain and accepted Killian's assault.

"Holy fucking hell!" Doug yelled, jerking his body as he fought to escape the burning pain that radiated from his anus. It felt like Killian was ripping his ass apart.

"Shh...calm down Doug. If you relax the pain will go away." Now it was Alana reassuring him, as his best friend stole his anal virginity—virginity that he never ever anticipated losing to anyone. What the hell had he done?

"He's killing me!" Doug whined, flexing his ass muscles around Killian's cock as he fought for comfort.

"No he's not. Push out as he takes you and it will be better." Alana murmured, stroking his face, and kissing his jaw. "Come on baby, you can take him. It's so fucking hot, knowing that he's fucking you while you're fucking me. God, that turns me on!"

She was still writhing on top of him and, now that he was focusing on something else, the pain was actually fading. Yet Killian still remained completely frozen, awaiting Doug's go-ahead. After a few seconds, Alana resumed her ride atop his now semi-hard cock, and his eyes were drawn to her jiggling breasts. Before long his cock thickened and he began to move with her again. That was when he realized he was fucking both of them at the same time.

His eyes shot to the space over her shoulder where he found Killian peering down at him, with a satisfied smirk on his handsome face.

"Now it's my turn to fuck you."

~ ~ ~

Killian…

That was the only warning Doug and Alana received before Killian pulled his cock almost completely out of Doug's virgin asshole, and slammed back into him in one solid thrust. It was a tight fit as all eight inches of Killian's stiff shaft stretched Doug's snug ring to the breaking point. It was hell on his control.

Killian's balls ached with the need to fill Doug with his cum, but he pushed it back. This moment was too important to let it slip through his fingers. Reaching out, he lifted Doug's hips higher so that he could get a better angle, and then shoved one of the fancy decorator throw pillows under him. It lifted him, and Alana enough that Killian could continue to thrust without holding them up.

Both of his hands sought out Alana, and he pulled her back up into a seated position. Doug had ceased his thrusting motion completely, and Alana clung to them limply, willing to play sex doll between them. Both of them were letting Killian drive their movement, and every time he slammed into Doug, it fucked all three of them.

His own fantasy fulfilled, Killian let himself relish in the naughty pleasures of the flesh. Squeezing Alana's bouncing tits, before reaching down to squeeze Doug's tight ass, rubbing his cock head hard against the top of Doug's passage so that he was putting distinct pressure on his prostate, and then easing back to give him a few of the sharper thrusts that Alana seemed to prefer. The three bodies made up one massive jigsaw puzzle that moved in glorious tandem, and brought them all to screaming orgasms, one after the other.

First Doug, whose entire body tightened around Killian, then Alana screamed and began shuddering violently. Her arms flailed until Killian grabbed them and pinned them to her sides. That only seemed to increase her pleasure, and she cried out again, this time begging.

"Fuck him. Fill him. I want you to fill him with your cum. Just like he did me."

That was the last thing Killian heard before the blood rushing through his ears shut off any other sound. His balls exploded, emptying every bit of passion he could muster deep inside Doug.

Chapter Seven

A lana...

The three bodies were collapsed in one massive heap on the bed, panting and sweating as they recovered from their aerobics. Doug was trembling under her cheek, and she could feel his heart racing behind his rib cage.

No one said a word. The only sounds were heavy breathing and the clock on the bedside table ticking away the seconds. The whole crazy night came crashing down on top of the three of them in that moment. Bliss faded as their passion waned, and they carefully separated their bodies.

Doug tugged her up into the crook of his arm, so that her cheek fit right into the curve of his shoulder, and she reached for Killian, hoping he would blanket her back. Her hand grasped nothing but air.

Killian had distanced himself from them already. He still lay in the bed, sprawled on his back, with one arm thrown over his eyes, but he might as well have been in another country for all the intimacy there was between them.

"Sir?" she asked, her voice hoarse from her passionate cries of pleasure. When he tensed but remained silent, she tried again, "Sir? Killian?"

He sat up, and shoved his hand through his hair, sighing heavily. "It's okay, Alana. The game's over; you don't have to call me Sir anymore."

After what they had just shared together, it was a slap in the face, and she hiccupped a sob of shock. "Killian, what's wrong?"

"Nothing, love. I'm fine. I'm just going to take a shower and let you two get some sleep. Doug you should probably soak in a tub at some point tonight or in the morning to give your sore muscles a rest." He rose to his full height at the edge of the bed, but he lingered indecisively. "I…uh…well, thanks for everything. I mean, thanks for tonight."

Four steps. That was as far as he got before she broke. She launched herself out of Doug's arms, grabbing Killian's hand and pulling him against her. Tears spilled hotly down her cheeks, and she shook her head against his broad chest as his hands stroked her naked back. "Don't do this, Killian."

"Don't do what, love? Did we hurt you? Come on, get up on the bed, and let me check you over. We were too rough with you, damn it." He was pushing her backward toward the bed.

"No, I'm fine, but I won't be if you leave. Why are you running away?" She let him push her down onto the bed, but he followed her because she still held his hand tightly in her grip, sinking to his knees.

"I'm just giving you guys some space, Alana. I went into this with open eyes and no expectations past tonight. I figured you would prefer me to give you some room to breathe after everything." He looked confused—and sad—and she wanted to wrap him tightly to her chest like she would a child to reassure and comfort him.

"No expectations?" Doug said, drawing both of their gazes back to him. He was sitting up on the side of the bed, watching them. His dark brown eyes held the same hurt and betrayal she felt in her heart.

Killian nodded, "You guys have been married a long time and you wanted to have a kinky night. It's okay, really. I just didn't want to overstay my welcome in your bed."

"Was that all this was to you? A kinky night?" Doug asked with a frown.

"What else could it be? I'm not exactly the commitment type. You of all people should know that." Killian shrugged, and rose to his feet slipping his hand from hers.

He sounded confident, but Alana could see the loneliness under his bravado, and she had no intention of letting him hide from them now. They had just shared each other's bodies, in ways that most friends never did. They had exposed themselves, and their hidden vulnerabilities. Now Killian was feeling weak, and unsure of his place with them.

Determined to make him see reason, Alana jumped back up to her feet and crossed her arms over her bare breasts, fighting the urge to stomp her foot in anger. "No! I saw you. I saw the real you, tonight, and I'll be damned if I'm going to let you pull on a mask of indifference again and walk around like we didn't just share something spectacular tonight."

~ ~ ~

Killian…

He desperately tried to school his features as he squared off against Alana. She was right. The whole evening had been spectacular, beyond anything he'd ever experienced, but that didn't mean he expected to suddenly be welcomed into their bed every night. It was just a fantasy. "It's not like that, Alana. I'm giving you space. I pushed you both out of your comfort zone tonight, and you need time to process."

"Exactly, Mr. Dominant. We need aftercare from our Dom." She bit the words out like venom, and he forced himself not to flinch in front of her.

"I'm not your Dom, Alana, but if you need me to hold you, I will. I'd love to, in fact, but it won't change the fact that I'm going to walk out that door when the sun rises," Killian said in a soft voice. He was torn between running from the room, and leaping back into the bed.

"We need you, Killian."

He shook his head, "You have a husband. You two love each other beyond all reason. I've seen you stare into each other's eyes a million times. I'm honored that you chose me to join you tonight. I won't lie; I've watched you come to these parties for months without even a hint of emotion, Alana. It made me crazy. That's why I touched you tonight, because I wasn't going to waste an opportunity to get my hands on you and crack your perfect outer shell, but I'm not a cuddler. I usually have other people attend to the aftercare for me, because I don't want the subs I play with to get too attached. You're different. So, if you need me to hold you. I will."

To Killian's surprise, Doug rose from the bed, and moved toward him confidently. His first steps were tentative, and Killian felt guilty knowing that he had taken his virginity so roughly. It wasn't his way. He was known for being tender and caring with his subs, but this pair had broken his control.

When he stood just inches away, Doug put his hand on the back of Killian's neck, and pulled his head down until they were barely a breath apart. "You know what I think? I think you're scared of how intimate tonight was. You're afraid of getting too close." Killian reared back trying to break free of the intimate hold, but Doug wasn't having it. "I may not be a Dom, but I know fear when I see it. You pushed our boundaries tonight, *Sir*," he spat out the title as an insult instead of a designation of respect, with an angry growl, "so I think turnabout's fair play. You're going to get into the bed, and provide the aftercare she needs. I may not know much, but I do know that you wouldn't have taken me…or Alana, if you weren't invested emotionally. Don't run now."

Killian looked from the door to Doug, to Alana, and back to the door. "I don't know how to do relationships, and you two have been married for an eternity…"

"Fifteen years is not an eternity." Alana said with a small laugh.

"It is when the longest relationship you ever had was a six-month affair in London with a woman who turned out to be married. We had a wild, wicked night; let it go at that."

Doug dropped his hand, and shrugged, "Fine, if you want it that way. I'll have the lawyers draw up the paperwork in the morning."

"What?" Killian's mouth gaped in shock and it felt like his heart stopped beating in his chest. Doug couldn't possibly mean what he said. "For what?"

"To separate our joint business ventures." Doug responded matter-of-factly.

Everything inside of Killian unraveled. He might not be able to be part of their marriage, but he wasn't ready to give up being part of their lives. "Why the hell would we do that?"

A sad smile spread across Doug's face, "Because I only do business with people I can trust not to betray me, and if you walk out that door right now, we're at the end of our friendship."

"Don't say that, Doug. You and Alana mean the world to me. Do you think I normally join threesomes with random married couples? Of course you mean something to me, but I'm not content with being the third wheel on this bicycle, and I'll be damned if I'll be some sort of sex toy that stays in the bedside table and only comes out once a month." Snapping his lips shut, Killian let out a growl of aggravation as he began to pace the room. They were quiet, but he could have sworn they were having a conversation. After a few moments, he stopped pacing and turned back to face them. They sat now, side by side on the bed, watching him evenly. Alana's lips curved up in a small, sexy smile, but Doug's face was absolutely emotionless.

When he spoke, his words were steady, but Doug's eyes told a different story. Every emotion possible shifted through them as he said something that nearly brought Killian to his knees. "In all my years I've never even been attracted to another man. Never been tempted to touch one, or taste one, and I sure as hell wouldn't have let any other man fuck me."

Killian flushed, and grimaced under Doug's frank attack. "I forced you."

"Maybe, but between Alana and I, I could have stopped you if I didn't want what you were giving me. Stop running, and step out of your comfort zone, Killian."

"Step out of my comfort zone, and what?"

Alana held out her hand, "And join us. For tonight, for tomorrow, for however long this arrangement makes all three of us happy."

He shook his head, but he was unable to keep from taking a step toward her. "I don't know how to do this."

"Come back to bed, and watch how it's done. We'll take care of you." Now Doug held his hand out. They wanted him. Not Killian the Dom, but Killian the man.

He stared at those two upturned hands for what seemed like hours, but could only have been moments. Alana's tiny pale white one with its petal soft skin was the complete opposite of Doug's larger callused palm, but they both offered the same thing. Killian reached for them. Perhaps it was time to push himself a little, and fulfill his own fantasies...

The End

Also By Lori King

Fetish & Fantasy
Watching Sin
Submission Dance
Mistress Hedonism
Masquerade

Crawley Creek Series
Beginnings
Forget Me Knot
Rough Ride Romeo
Claiming His Cowgirl
Hawke's Salvation (Coming January 2016)

The Gray Pack Series
Fire of the Wolf
Reflections of the Wolf
Legacy of the Wolf
Dreams of the Wolf
Caress of the Wolf
Honor of the Wolf

The Surrender Trilogy
Weekend Surrender
Flawless Surrender
Primal Surrender
Broken Surrender (Coming November 2015)

Apache Crossing
Sidney's Triple Shot

Sunset Point
Point of Seduction

Anthologies
Irrevocably Claimed
Tempting Tanner

About the Author

Best-selling author, Lori King, is also a full-time wife and mother of three boys. Although she rarely has time to just enjoy feminine pursuits; at heart she is a hopeless romantic. She spends her days dreaming up Alpha men, and her nights telling their stories. An admitted TV and book junkie, she can be found relaxing with a steamy story, or binging in an entire season of some show online. She gives her parents all the credit for her unique sense of humor and acceptance of all forms of love. There are no two loves alike, but you can love more than one with your whole heart.

With the motto: Live, Laugh, and Love like today is your only chance, she will continue to write as long as you continue to read. Thank you for taking the time to indulge in a good Happily Ever After with her. Find out more about her current projects at http://lorikingbooks.com, or look her up on Facebook: http://www.facebook.com/LoriKingBooks or Twitter: https://twitter.com/LoriKingBooks.